KGB

UNTOLD HISTORY OF SOVIET'S INTELLIGENCE & SECRET FORCE

N. CHOKKAN

PRABHAT
PRAKASHAN

Published by
PRABHAT PRAKASHAN PVT. LTD.
4/19 Asaf Ali Road,
New Delhi-110 002 (INDIA)
e-mail: prabhatbooks@gmail.com

ISBN 978-93-5562-557-1

KGB – UNTOLD HISTORY OF SOVIET'S INTELLIGENCE & SECRET FORCE
by N. Chokkan

Edition
First, 2024

Price
₹ 300 (Rupees Three Hundred Only)

Printed at
Sita Fine Arts, Delhi

Dedicated to
Thiru. Rajaraman 'anna'...

Author's Note

For much of the 20th century, the Soviet Union was veiled behind an Iron Curtain of secrecy and oppression orchestrated by the Communist party and intelligence services like the KGB. While the public knew of the KGB as a spy agency abroad, few glimpsed its extensive surveillance and suppression of dissent within Soviet borders. And with the fall of the Soviet Union in 1991, the full extent of its clandestine activities may have vanished from memory.

Yet piecing together defectors' accounts, recovered records, and investigative journalism is beginning to unravel some of the most sensational intrigues traced back to KGB headquarters. This book peels back the curtain on the covert operations that gripped global attention during the Cold War era between the capitalist West and communist East. But it also surfaces new findings on the KGB's covert assignments that influenced generations behind the Iron Curtain.

Russia has long employed extrajudicial security forces for state protection, tracing back to Ivan the Terrible's oprichnina corps in the 16th century. But it was through the KGB and predecessor agencies that spycraft, subversion, and control were systematically implemented with chilling efficacy. At its peak, over 500,000 KGB employees and informants kept dissent and demonstrations at bay while conducting espionage across swathes of human society.

These pages document heart-stopping accounts of KGB assassination teams, infiltration operations, staged provocations, planted propaganda, and the capture of double agents abroad. But they also uncover widespread interference in culture, media, religion, and daily life behind the Soviet border. Such findings compel an unsettling reassessment of an agency ruling through orchestrated fear rather than overt public accountability.

The aim is not just to recount historical events but to offer an inside story—a perspective that goes beyond the superficial understanding of covert operations. It is an exploration of the motivations, the betrayals, and the sacrifices made by those who operated in the shadows, shaping the course of history with every classified mission.

❑

Contents

1
A Twelve-year Penance

The doors and windows of the room were tightly shut. Not even the wind could enter into the fortification.

He was reading a few documents in the dimly lit and stuffy atmosphere. After reading each document, he thought for a few minutes. Then, he placed the document in one of the few files that were placed before him and noted down the information on a sheet of paper.

Most of the documents present in that room were discoloured and disfigured with age. But the contents of those papers were still alive. Several emotions—success, failure, hope, treachery, fatigue, greed, lust, desire, pride, hate, fear, bravery and others were filled in those papers. Those papers were the remnants of which had directly or indirectly changed the history of several nations.

Almost all the documents were marked 'top-secret'. Hardly anyone would have read any of those documents after they had been written. Nobody would have read all the secrets that had accumulated for more than half a decade.

The old man realised that no other human on this earth could imagine the golden opportunity that he had got. He decided to utilise it properly.

He thought that the secrets and historical events should not be buried inside a dark room forever. While people thought they knew their nation, its policies, leaders and groups, like how a blind man would have understood the appearance of an elephant, the harsh truth should be recorded somehow.

He thought that the secrets and historical events should not be buried inside a dark room forever. While people thought they knew their nation, its policies, leaders and groups, like how a blind man would have understood the appearance of an elephant, the harsh truth should be recorded somehow.

He did not have the answer for 'how and when' to do it. When he thought about his fate if somebody came to know about his plans, he shuddered.

But nothing affected his work. He started making arrangements to reveal the truth hidden in the documents to the outside world. His office was moving to a new location then. His duty was to take all the documents safely from the old office to the new office.

He went to the archives room in the old office each Wednesday and read the notes. After reading them for hours together, he rearranged them based on their time period or title and bundled them together. Those bundles were placed in huge boxes or containers and were sealed under his supervision. The next day, all those boxes were taken to the new office. He had to make sure of it personally.

His duty did not end with that. He had to receive all the boxes in the new office, account for them properly and had to arrange them in order.

Likewise, he was carefully transporting lakhs and lakhs of secret documents by working two days a week in the old office and three days a week in the new office. The papers which he handled during this period had several international secrets, their severity ranging from tiny crackers to atom bombs. When those secrets were leaked someday, there would not be a country on the map which would not be affected by them.

A huge danger was involved in taking whole sheets of paper outside, so he decided to take notes in small pieces of paper and smuggle them out. But that plan also had a flaw. If somebody suspected something and checked him out someday, he would be caught red-handed with pen and paper.

Would somebody trust an individual to handle such sensitive and important documents?

They had. The geniuses who interfered in everybody else's affairs for more than seventy five years, trusted an old man and handed over all their information to him. That old man who was trusted by everybody decided to take the secrets out to the world and was searching for ways to do that.

Although there were no Tehelka examples and micro cameras during that period, he was working for the number one 'spies' of the entire world. He had read all their adventures that were written down. Wouldn't he find a way?

He started with an easy way at the beginning. He remembered all the points which he read each day and noted it down when he reached home in the evening. That was a neat and easy way which nobody could detect. But, how much could he remember at his age? Moreover, many contained long twisted Russian names which were difficult to remember.

He decided after a few weeks that his method would not work. He started to make another plan. A huge danger was involved in taking whole sheets of paper outside, so he decided to take notes in small pieces of paper and smuggle them out. But that plan also had a flaw. If somebody suspected something and checked him out someday, he would be caught red-handed with pen and paper.

He thought that the secrets and historical events should not be buried inside a dark room forever. While people thought they knew their nation, its policies, leaders and groups, like how a blind man would have understood the appearance of an elephant, the harsh truth should be recorded somehow.

He thought of a plan for that. He took notes in small bits of paper, then threw them in the dustbin. In this way, information would be copied and he would be in less danger. He filled the dustbin with crumpled paper all day. In the evening, he collected those papers, straightened them, hid them inside his socks and walked back home.

A few weeks went by. Nobody suspected that he was hiding something in his socks every day. Nobody checked him even for a formality. Since all the major officers had already shifted to the new building, security arrangements were less in the document storage area. Once in a while, a few were stopped and their bags were checked. But nobody was checked personally.

After making sure of this security lapse, his confidence increased. He started to place the secret papers in his pockets instead of his socks. He arranged the papers which he smuggled from his office at his home and at his holiday houses called the 'dacha'. When he had time, he typed and compiled the information together. The information was then buried underground.

While he was doing it, he was not sure if those papers would be unearthed someday or if they would be buried forever. But he considered it his duty to compile and safeguard the information. He worked with the same fervour and compiled important information.

He did persistently not do it for just a year or two. He worked persistently for twelve years. Until he retired from his work in 1984, his secret mission continued. The twelve-year penance was known to the world only fifteen years later when an earthquake erupted all over the world at the same time. Whenever the name KGB is uttered, the old man's name, Vasili Mitrokhin is also said aloud.

❑

2
The Dog and the Broom

Officially, KGB was a group which was created in Soviet Union in 1954 and which was dissolved in 1991. Its lifetime did not cross forty years.

But, the term KGB collectively refers to other clandestine police and intelligence groups of the Soviet Union before and after that time frame.

For example, here is a small list:

- Cheka (1917–1922)
- GPU or State Political Directorate (1922–1923)
- OGPU or Joint State Political Directorate (1923–1934)
- GUGB or Main Directorate for State Security (1934–1941)
- NKGB People's Commissariat for State Security (1941, 1943–1946)

- GUGB Main Directorate for State Security (1941–1943)
- MGB Ministry of State Security (1946–1947)
- KI Committee of Information (1947–1951)
- MVD Ministry of Internal Affairs (1953–1954)
- KGB Committee for State Security (1954–1991)

When the Russian revolution ended and the Bolshevik government was formed in 1917, Cheka was formed. Later, when the Soviet Union was shattered into pieces in 1991, Cheka operated under various names and held high influence.

All of the above list are various avatars of KGB. Although the list of KGB's avatars extends like Vishnu's avatars, all of them had similar missions, methods, people, love and hatred they gained among the public.

When the Russian revolution ended and the Bolshevik government was formed in 1917, Cheka was formed. Later, when the Soviet Union was shattered into pieces in 1991, Cheka operated under various names and held high influence.

Leaders changed, generations changed, people's mentality changed, politics, economy, culture, art, literature and everything changed within that time period. But a few things stood high amidst all the changes around them—one was 'communism' and another was 'KGB' alias 'Cheka.

It is not fair to compare Soviet's intelligence agency to a clandestine police group. But, how else to refer to the group which was formed as a 'temporary solution' by the comrades and later was pampered as their brainchild?

Let us look at what is Cheka and what was the reason behind its formation before analysing about it.

To understand the reason behind Cheka, we should travel five and half centuries behind.

Russia was ruled by Ivan IV at that period. He was the first person who took the title 'Tsar' and is referred to as 'Ivan the Terrible' by the history books. He is portrayed with a huge beard and angry eyes in most of the pictures.

If he was named as 'terrible', we can imagine how cruel he would have been. But there were people who did not fear Ivan even then. Ivan, who hated them, plotted a cruel way to destroy them altogether.

Ivan formed a personal security force for him named Oprichiniki. The primary task of this force was to protect the great Ivan from others. The Oprichiniki were the pioneers to the special forces who protect present-day politicians. In addition to protecting the emperor, they killed all those who were the king's enemies and prospective enemies.

Ivan formed a personal security force for him named Oprichiniki. The primary task of this force was to protect the great Ivan from others. The Oprichiniki were the pioneers to the special forces who protect present-day politicians. In addition to protecting the emperor, they killed all those who were the king's enemies and prospective enemies.

We know about enemies, but who were the prospective enemies?

They were those who raised their voice against the king and those who instigated people to riot against the king. Oprichiniki found them and punished them. They captured many people on the pretext that they might act against the king in the future. There was no scientific information-based research to find those who acted against the king. They captured everybody as per their wish.

That is, Oprichiniki could brand anybody as a prospective enemy and arrest them. They could punish them without any enquiry. Punishment did not mean whippings or standing in cold water. The only punishment they had was death sentence. Oprichiniki made sure that nobody had the courage to oppose the king in any way.

Due to their ruthless cruelty, people were terrified of the Oprichiniki. They were unsure of who might be their next target and for what reason. Ivan chose a uniform for the Oprichiniki to portray their cruelty. They were dressed in jet black and rode black horses like the envoys of death, killing all the rebellious thoughts of the public. Just like their uniform, Ivan chose a debatable emblem for the Oprichiniki. It had the image of a dog and a broom.

Oprichiniki's actions matched their emblem. They sniffed out all who opposed Ivan and swept them aside like filth. Ivan made sure that everybody feared his security force. He personally interviewed all the members before recruitment.

What is the relation between a dog and a broom?

Dogs sniff out those who do rebellious deeds. Brooms sweep them away like dust. Which other image could symbolise the king's protection force better than this?

Oprichiniki's actions matched their emblem. They sniffed out all who opposed Ivan and swept them aside like filth. Ivan made sure that everybody feared his security force. He personally interviewed all the members before recruitment.

All those who were recruited had to take an oath in front of the emperor. They had to promise that despite any obstacle they might face, they had to slay the emperor's enemies without any hesitation. Only after that they would receive their black uniform.

Ivan had almost six thousand members in his Oprichiniki force. Many murders, riots and cruelties occurred in the country due to them.

There is information about several other kings who had a personal security force to ensure their safety. The duty of these forces were to safeguard the king and his family members. It was considered a challenging task in those days when political murders were of common occurrence.

Whenever the king or his family members stepped out to go wherever they wanted to go, the security force members would follow them. If any situation arose, they would have to protect the royal family by sacrificing their own lives.

Alexander II was born in 1818, became the Tsar in his thirty-seventh year. Several enemies mushroomed against him all over the country within the next few years. In April 1866, the first attempt was made against his life.

Do you get the image of reading a historical novel with security forces and horses? That is right! Several security forces including the Oprichiniki were primarily involved in such security tasks.

Their secondary task was intelligence work. They found out who talked or acted against the king, spied on them finding out their mission and made plans to spoil their plots. The existence of the 'secret police' force started from that point.

The security force thus became an indispensable part of the Tsar government. Their importance rose again during the nineteenth century. The reason for their rise was Tsar Alexander II.

Alexander II was born in 1818, became the Tsar in his thirty-seventh year. Several enemies mushroomed against him all over the country within the next few years. In April 1866, the first attempt was made against his life. A man named Dmitry Karakazov tried to shoot down the Tsar when he was at the gates of his summer place in St. Petersberg. Luckily, the Tsar escaped it.

Alexander believed that the Almighty saved him from the attack. Hence, he ordered his people to build prayer halls in all the churches of his kingdom to celebrate his escape. Along with it, he wanted to find those who made an attempt against his life and punish them severely. He formed a group of twelve members in St. Petersburg to find them. It was named the 'Department on Securing the Order and Public Peace'. It was aimed at maintaining order and peace among the public.

> *On 1st March 1881, a group of five men surrounded Alexander on all sides and killed him using explosives. This incident started terrorist activities all over the world and created a huge stir in Russia. It raised a question all over the country—how to find and manage anti-Tsar and anti-government rebels?*

When somebody has attempted to kill the ruler, it meant that law and order has been disrupted in that country. It was believed that the new group would find those responsible for the disruption and right the wrong. But this group did not aim at solving the law-and-order crisis by looking into the basic needs of the people. Instead, it was yearning to find those who tried to kill the king and to castigate them.

Due to their attitude, there was no significant growth in Russia during the reign of Alexander II. There was only hatred and loathing among the public. People who were angry with their governing system started a revolutionary group named Narodnaya Volya which meant 'people's power'. The primary mission of this group was to kill the Tsar.

A student tried to assassinate the Tsar in April 1879. In December 1879 and February 1880, the Narodnaya Volya organised bombings to murder the Tsar, but he escaped from all the attempts without a scratch on him. The Tsar was not sure of how long his luck would safeguard him. But he understood something clearly, that the group which he formed to protect him was not of much use and that the people wanted to kill with more vehemence than before.

Hence, Alexander II decided to form a more secure protective force to manage the situation. Accordingly, the Department of State Police was formed. They had more power than the older group and they searched all over Russia for the troublemakers.

The irony was that although it was a brilliant idea, the second force failed to protect Alexander's life.

On 1st March 1881, a group of five men surrounded Alexander on all sides and killed him using explosives.

This incident started terrorist activities all over the world and created a huge stir in Russia. It raised a question all over the country—how to find and manage anti-Tsar and anti-government rebels?

This question troubled the next Tsar, Alexander III. He was worried that he might also face numerous attempts on his life like the previous Tsar. His fears soon proved valid, and attempts to kill him started soon. The police force which was formed a year before, could not control the revolutionaries.

Alexander III decided to make additional protective measures and started to open special security centres in several parts of his kingdom. These security centres which were opened for the first time in Moscow and Warsaw can be considered the pioneers of current day police stations. The name which was given to these centres during the reign of Alexander III was 'Security and Investigation Secret Police Stations'.

A major change happened in the thought process of the rulers due to this arrangement. The security force which aimed to protect the Tsar should not only follow the ruler with firearms; they had to observe the happenings inside the country, the public's opinion about the rule, any riots that happened so far and their after effects and the means to control further riots. Only when all this information was known, could they nip it in the bud.

Alexander III understood the strategy and started to open more police stations to observe people in various parts of his country. These stations grew gradually and acquired several other responsibilities in the later years. This police force which operated from 1881 until the end of the Russian Tsars in 1917 were not as cruel as their predecessor, Oprichiniki. But still they instilled a fear in the hearts of people and protected the Tsars and their families.

They can be considered as the great grandfather of later KGB and was known as Okhrana.

❑

3
Eyes on the Back

The full name of Okhrana was *Otdeleniye po Okhraneniyu* which meant 'Department of Protection' or 'the Guard Department'.

The Okhrana which stepped into the field directly were given a few crucial responsibilities based on the previous events and experiences.

1. Protecting the Tsar and his family.
2. Finding out riots and disruptions before they occured and suppressing them.

There was nothing new in their list, the tasks were just the same as those of the police force. But, due to the significant political and social changes that happened in Russia at the end of the nineteenth century, Okhrana had to tackle several new challenges.

For example, the factory workers of Russia who completed their work without a murmur so far, started to protest asking for added benefits, more wages and to reduce their work burden (they were working for more than 14 hours a day).

From 1895, several protests, strikes and gripes happened in Russia with several demands.

The owner of a factory is similar to the king of a nation. If somebody has the courage to oppose a factory's owner, they will not hesitate to oppose a king too.

More than anything else, the Tsarist government wanted to suppress the Marxist groups which gained importance all over Russia by the end of the nineteenth century. Okhrana officers started their plan to implement the Tsar's orders.

The Tsars understood it and got alerted. They clearly defined the scope of Okhrana in various parts of the government.

1. Finding out workers' protests and preventing them.
2. Buying or silencing the leaders of the workers who rebel against them.
3. Finding out if there is opposition against the government outside the factories.
4. Identifying traitors.

More than anything else, the Tsarist government wanted to suppress the Marxist groups which gained importance all over Russia by the end of the nineteenth century. Okhrana officers started their plan to implement the Tsar's orders.

Okhrana decided that the first step that had to be taken was to look into the workers' protest which was the root cause of every problem. They launched their security centres in the cities where there were a greater number of factories and where the factory workers lived predominantly like St. Petersburg, Moscow and Warsaw.

The primary goal of these security centres was to penetrate into the workers' circle and to find out what they had in their mind.

Okhrana did not use uniformed policemen to execute this plan, instead, they employed a few local workers for the task. They can be rightly called spies rather than workers. Their only task was to pretend interest in the workers' groups/unions, find their inside information and then report it to Okhrana.

The workers were compensated well for the successful completion of their job. Since they received huge amounts which they had never seen before in their lives, they were faithful to Okhrana.

During the same time, Okhrana followed another strategy too. A few of Okhrana's officers/ agents started to become close to the union leaders of the workers' groups. They were able to get to know several secrets directly through them. They also had a rare opportunity to brainwash the protestors' leaders too.

During the same time, Okhrana followed another strategy too. A few of Okhrana's officers/agents started to become close to the union leaders of the workers' groups. They were able to get to know several secrets directly through them. They also had a rare opportunity to brainwash the protestors' leaders too.

They employed several statements such as 'How noble our king is. He has showered us with numerous presents. We have enjoyed his generosity for so many years, is it fair to forget everything and protest against him? Shouldn't we be fair?'

But, would the union leaders be mollified with such saccharine words? Workers' rights were not a luxury. Okhrana did not understand that rights are the basic needs of the workers. So, Okhrana's measures to brainwash the leaders, buying them with money and other comforts did not yield them much success. The red flag of remonstration was raised higher in Russia.

Although the 1905 revolution which shook Russia did not succeed, it sent a shiver down the spine of the Tsar's lineage. They understood that their enemies would crush them completely if they got a chance. They wanted to act before their enemies di. The Okhrana centres which were located sparsely until then increased in number all over Russia. It was proportional with the rise in the number of revolutionary groups.

Okhrana started to target revolutionary leaders and communist leaders then. Their primary goal was to stop the riots and protests against Tsars even before they started. Okhrana representatives started to mingle with the disgruntled public and started to gain their trust, gradually. Their goal was to relay every minor information against the Tsar to their head office.

When compared to Okhrana's previous attempts, this tactic gave them more success. Two factors can be claimed as the reason for this success.

Okhrana agents who were using age-old practices so far were trained on modern spying and intelligence tactics. The agents got formal training and became experts in gathering information without tipping off their opponents. Moreover, Okhrana did not rely upon its employees alone. It had the fantastic idea to buy spies if needed.

First factor, Okhrana's Moscow wing leader, Sergei Zubatov was involved in modernizing Okhrana's activities from 1895. Sergei introduced several new innovations in Okhrana including basic things like saving all the details about the suspects in a single file so that they could be accessed easily, using photographic tools to gather secrets and forming a special squad for emergency situations.

Okhrana agents who were using age-old practices so far were trained on modern spying and intelligence tactics. The agents got formal training and became experts in gathering information without tipping off their opponents. Moreover, Okhrana did not rely upon its employees alone. It had the fantastic idea to buy spies if needed.

For example, consider a revolutionary group which is very secretive. It might be difficult for Okhrana agents to infiltrate into it, reach the leaders and to gain their trust. In such situations, instead of breaking their heads to enter into it, they pulled already existing members who were close to the leaders on their side.

The plan might look simple at first glance. But it had many challenges while implementing in the real world. Okhrana had several tricks in their bag to execute it.

The first trick was money. Based on the position of the person who was willing to spy for Okhrana, heavy compensation was given ranging from hundred rubles to thousands. When compared to the average wage a Russian worker earned in that period, it was a jackpot. The luxury and comfort that could be bought from the extra money attracted many.

Okhrana did the same. They informed the prisoners that they were released and free to go home. They cruelly stared at the happiness the prisoners had on their faces. They then revealed the catch in their announcement, "But, if you want to be free, you have to do us a favour."

But, can everybody be bought with money?

Okhrana had realised the answer to this question earlier through experience. Hence, they decided to make use of 'fear' on those who were not attracted to money. They monitored the leaders, commanders and secondary commanders closely. When they committed a misdeed or an illegal activity, they were arrested by Okhrana.

The captives of Okhrana were given severe punishments during that period. The punishments which ranged from solidtary confinement in Siberian prisons till death sentence scared even the bravest of hearts.

All those who were arrested by Okhrana would be prepared for enduring severe torture. What if they were informed that they would not face any torture and will be released the next day?

Okhrana did the same. They informed the prisoners that they were released and free to go home. They cruelly stared at the happiness the prisoners had on their faces. They then revealed the catch in their announcement, "But, if you want to be free, you have to do us a favour."

The favour was to spy on the revolutionaries and to send important information to Okhrana officers. Many bluntly refused to be a part of such treachery. They would then be threatened with many cruelties.

"Think well, we are ready to forgive your crimes and release you, willing to pay you a hefty amount even. Won't you do this small favour for us?" This would be their question.

A few revolutionaries understood that it was their last chance to live. They gave up their policies and values and joined hands with Okhrana.

But, what was the guarantee that they would act in favour of Okhrana after their release? They could not be controlled by Okhrana after their release. Okhrana found a way to keep them in line even after their release. They got a written statement from them accepting all their crimes. Only after that, they made their offer.

Due to this statement, none of those who accepted to help Okhrana could change track later. If they wanted to change, Okhrana threatened them with the statement. If needed, they were arrested again, thrown into prison and were tortured with new innovative techniques.

The 'turned-spies' understood their fate clearly and were mostly loyal to Okhrana. Due to their cooperation, Okhrana received up to date information about the revolutionary groups.

During that period, Okhrana's direct and indirect agents had infiltrated almost all the revolutionary and political groups. A few of them even rose pivotal positions in those groups.

For example, Evno Azef, one of the leaders of Socialist Revolutionary Party (SR) and Roman Malinovsky of Bolshevik Party worked as Okhrana agents. There is an unconfirmed rumour that Joseph Stalin who was one of the major leaders of Bolshevik

Party and who was later the president of Russia worked as an Okhrana agent during his initial days.

Okhrana had made a separate file on Stalin since he was involved in various revolutionary acts and was a popular leader. But crucial information in that file has disappeared. There are a few who argue that Stalin himself had destroyed that information as he did not want 'old' information about him to be revealed after he became the president of the Soviet Union.

But what was the secret that Stalin wanted to hide badly?

In 1956, *Life* magazine released a letter regarding this. It was a letter written by Colonel Alexander Mikhailovich Eremin from St. Petersburg police station to a person named Alexi Fedorovich. In that letter, Eremin had commended an Okhrana agent named Joseph Vissarionovich. It was the real name of Stalin.

The letter mentioned that Stalin continued to send important information to Okhrana from 1908. It said that he started to act against the government at a certain point and then the connection between him and Okhrana was severed. No other document was retrieved so far to prove the information to be valid. So, it is unproved if the letter is genuine or was manipulated.

Although Stalin's association with Okhrana cannot be confirmed, it can be said that Okhrana had its spying eyes on several revolutionary groups of that period.

But, were those preventive measures able to suppress the Russian revolution?

❑

4
Okhrana

There were several secret organisations, groups and parties during the beginning of the twentieth century which operated in Russia with a revolutionary purpose in their mind. Although each of them had different policies, beliefs and approach, they all had a single 'common enemy'.

The common enemy was the Tsar who governed them cruelly. They wanted the Tsarist government and the other groups which supported him to be overthrown. They wanted a government for the people and by the people.

While the radical groups were struggling towards reaching their goal, the group which was formed to identify them and control them was Okhrana.

Okhrana and the radical groups hated each other. While Okhrana was trying to crush all the radical groups, the revolutionaries discussed ways to evade Okhrana agents. The revolutionary groups knew that a few Okhrana agents had infiltrated their trusted group. But they were unable to find who those black sheep were. At that time, somebody gave them a brilliant idea.

They knew that Okhrana was spying on them. They were unable to prevent them. What if they used the same weapon against Okhrana?

Does that mean spying upon Okhrana? Wasn't that absurd?

Although this 'double agent' plan is an age-old plan in the present world, it gained huge success in those days against Okhrana. According to Okhrana, they got regular information about the radical groups. But, they did not realise that that information was of no use.

There was no point in the revolutionaries spying on Okhrana. But, what about distracting them with false or ambiguous information?

That is, a few of the revolutionaries went to Okhrana on the pretext that they were ready to assist them. Okhrana welcomed them with open arms and added them to their spy network. After gaining Okhrana's trust, the revolutionaries gave false information to Okhrana. The fee they got for their information was used to develop their own groups.

Although this 'double agent' plan is an age-old plan in the present world, it gained huge success in those days against Okhrana. According to Okhrana, they got regular information about the radical groups. But, they did not realise that that information was of no use.

While they planned preventive measures in one part of the country based on their secret, information, the revolutionaries executed their plans in another part of the country without any disturbances.

Since Okhrana's enemies squandered their time and their reputation in the government, their image started to get tarnished gradually. Until then, there were Okhrana centres in several parts of the Tsar's kingdom. Apart from them, they had centres in foreign nations including Paris and London to capture the revolutionaries who were hiding in those countries.

Okhrana's actions were criticised severely after 1910. Moreover, they lost their credence completely due to the false information given by the double agents.

Due to this, several Okhrana centres were closed. In 1917 ,when the Russian revolution was at its peak, only a few Okhrana centres were active, that too mostly by name.

The important criminals arrested by Okhrana were handed over to the law department. Okhrana had to provide help to run the case against them. These included several tasks which wasted Okhrana agents' time including preparing legal documents, getting the evidence ready, participating in case enquiries and providing the needed information and several others.

Okhrana had the responsibility of preventing the protests against the Tsars as one among its priorities. Although it was functioning in the right direction, it never grew into a major organisation. It did not have a separate army, and the modern intelligence techniques used by them were not sufficient to act against people's revolution.

One other major setback for Okhrana's existence was that they only had the power to arrest somebody. Running a case against them, punishing or freeing them were not under Okhrana's jurisdiction. The Russian department of law took care of those actions.

The important criminals arrested by Okhrana were handed over to the law department. Okhrana had to provide help to run the case against them. These included several tasks which wasted Okhrana agents' time including preparing legal documents, getting the evidence ready, participating in case enquiries and providing the needed information and several others.

The radical groups watched everything. When they started a security/intelligence group for themselves, they made sure to avoid such time-consuming activities. They gave enough power to them and made sure they functioned with complete authority.

It is not clear if the revolutionaries planned to eliminate Okhrana during the Russian revolution or if they lost their importance gradually with time. Anyway, Okhrana was in a weak state when the need for it was high. The Marxist brothers never ignored the Okhrana. Yet, while the Russian revolution was at its peak, they had several other important tasks to do.

Marxism which was an unknown political idea until the beginning of the twentieth century, gradually found its roots in Russia and led to a great revolt in 1917. Government groups including Okhrana could not do anything against this revolt. At the end, the Tsar government which ruled Russia for several generations came to an end with the last Tsar Nicholas II.

One of the most prominent people who was leading the Bolshevik group during the Russian revolution was Lenin. His full name was Vladimir Ilyich Ulyanov Lenin. Lenin read various political and Marxist books given by his brother Alexander right from his childhood. He had witnessed the exploitation and oppression by the Tsarist government. He developed a severe hatred toward it. In the year 1892, he studied law and started the first Marxist group in Russia. Lenin attracted not only the workers but also the common people through his writings and speech. He ran his party based on his policies and ignited an entire generation through it.

Marxism which was an unknown political idea until the beginning of the twentieth century, gradually found its roots in Russia and led to a great revolt in 1917. Government groups including Okhrana could not do anything against this revolt. At the end, the Tsar government which ruled Russia for several generations came to an end with the last Tsar Nicholas II.

Lenin and his comrades promised that the communist government would be entirely different from the previous government of the Tsars. The difference was not only in name, there were changes in the basic structure of the government too. Bolshevik government did not rule the people from the top; they announced that each one was a king and the resources would be available to everybody equally.

It meant that the Bolshevik government which was present then under Lenin's leadership was a temporary arrangement. Once the initial troubles were solved and the people's government was stabilised, people would rule themselves and they would not require a government to rule them.

When there would be no government, what about Okhrana?

The Bolshevik comrades claimed that they were not required. They believed that police, Okhrana, legal spies, arrest, enquiries, punishments and every other symbol of the previous government's oppression would disappear in course of time.

When everybody gets everything and lives prosperously under communist rule, nobody will steal from the others. Nobody will disrupt the lives of others. There will be nothing like crime, cases, robbery or murders. Since each person is a king, there would be no chance of revolts against the king.

Bolshevik highlighted several reasons like the above and claimed that there would be no need for the existence of a group like Okhrana. Lenin himself has written that 'there is no need for political police or secret police in people's rule'.

In that case, did Lenin believe that the new government would not face any opposition from anybody?

No, Lenin had good experience in politics and hence he knew that all new policies and governing methods would have some opposition. But he believed that communism had the answers to all the questions.

He strongly believed that although a few might oppose the rule in the beginning, they would realise that communism was the best policy in course of time and then would embrace it.

> *But the reality was not so smooth in Russia which was under his Bolshevik rule in 1917. Everybody was happy that the Tsarist government had come to an end. But comments were made against the new government and their policies which came into effect after the downfall of the Tsars.*

Though Lenin's beliefs are wonderful to hear. But the reality was not so smooth in Russia which was under his Bolshevik rule in 1917. Everybody was happy that the Tsarist government had come to an end. But comments were made against the new government and their policies which came into effect after the downfall of the Tsars.

When does a 'people's leader' who comes to power with majority of public support face opposition? Russia had several parties with various policies. In that case, how could the Bolsheviks take control of the entire government?

The parliamentary election which are conducted in 1917, the Bolshevik Party got less than twenty five percent votesAnd the Socialist Revolutionary Party won almost half of the total votes.

But Lenin dissolved the parliament after the election and announced that the Bolsheviks would rule them forever. This raised commotion all over the country. There was confusion if those disruptions were strong and if people really supported Lenin.

Although a new government was formed in Russia but there were minor and major troubles all over the country. It became necessary to observe the murmurs, predict their severity and take sufficient action against them. A group named 'Worker's and

Peasant's Militsiya' was formed under the Russian Internal Affairs Department.

What does Militsiya mean ?

'Militsiya' meant police/protective force in the Russian language. The new group's duty was to observe all the activities against the new government and protect the government from any major trouble. It was an interesting irony that the communist comrades who strongly believed that police force was not necessary in people's rule, formed a special police force within a short time after rising to power.

But Lenin did not have time to think about it then. At last the tyrannical rule by the Tsars had come to an end . He did not want to allow the growth of capitalists and any attempts made by them to capture the government before stabilising the communist rule. So, he wanted to find all the small and big groups which planned to overpower the new rule and to remove them. He created the Militsiya and looked for talented people to be a part of this group.

Lenin came to know about a revolutionary named Felix who was a member of the party. He played an important part in the February revolution of 1917. Lenin decided that Felix was the right person to run the new security force based on his qualifications and reputation. Then started the most important chapter in the history of Russia.

❑

5

A Bit of Moon and Fire

When somebody says 'Ironman' of India, it will immediately come to our mind 'Sardar Vallabhai Patel'. Likewise, Russians consider Felix as their ironman.

Although his full name was Felix Edmundovich Dzerzhinsky, he was fondly called 'Iron Felix'. The honesty and strictness that he showed in his job earned him the nickname, 'Iron felix'.

Felix was born on 11th September 1877 in an upper middle-class Polish family. He was religious during his childhood and when he grew up he wanted to become a Christian pastors.

But the reality was different.During his school days he was attracted toward revolutionary concepts.and enrolled himself in a local radical group. He was involved in several protests condemning oppression. Felix's relatives, friends and teachers advised him against all the political activities he was a part of since he was a little boy then,but Felix did not listen to anybody.

Then the school management decided that having Felix in their school would badly influence other students Since he was involved in revolutionary activities so the management dismissed Felix from the school. Felix was not bothered by his expulsion. In fact, he was happy about it since there would not be any more disturbances from his teachers, and he could involve himself in protests and strikes without any hindrance.

So, Felix would start to plan for his escape from the prison, every time he entered it. He found a way each time and escaped from the prison every time he was imprisoned. The police department was frustrated at his continuous escapes and sent him to a Siberian prison once in 1897 and again in 1900. But Felix managed to escape from the Siberian prison on both occasions.

When Felix was eighteen years old he joined a Marxist group then after a few years he joined a new group named 'Lithuanian Social Revolutionary Group'. His life underwent a massive upheaval after that. Felix was arrested several times after that on the grounds that he was involved in anti-social activities and spent a major part of his youth in prison. In truth, his prison life structured his political thoughts. His revolutionary ideals were intensified.

But who would take care of the group's activities if Felix was in prison? So, Felix would start to plan for his escape from the prison, every time he entered it. He found a way each time and escaped from the prison every time he was imprisoned.

The police department was frustrated at his continuous escapes and sent him to a Siberian prison once in 1897 and again in 1900. But Felix managed to escape from the Siberian prison on both occasions. He led a life in hiding for some years after that. In 1905, Felix participated in the revolution. When the revolution failed, he was imprisoned again.

He was not arrested by the ordinary police force but by the Okhrana which was determined to crush all the revolutionaries. For all his misdemeanours they granted severe punishment to Felix. Felix experienced a long sentence in jail for the first time in his life. He did not worry about his fate, but he started to write his detailed experience in jail in his journal.

> *Felix had protests as his life and led a hidden life all throughout. If he came out of his hiding, he was in danger of being captured by Okhrana. Felix who was arrested in 1905 by the Okhrana was released in 1912. Before he could enjoy his freedom he was again caught and imprisoned in Moscow. Felix was imprisoned for five years and was released in February 1917.*

His journal entries written from Warsaw prison was later released as a book named '*Prison Diary and Letters'*. The readers who read the book with its gentle words holding strong principles will imagine Felix to be a soft person. Nobody can imagine him as a rough revolutionary or as a strict police officer.

It was true that a romantic poet who enjoys each moment of his life was hidden inside Felix. But, at the same time, he had a bit of fire along with his soft nature. It made him operate as a professional revolutionist.

The term 'professional revolutionist' might look like a word written in humour, but, in those days in Russia, there were people who considered revolution as a profession and there was a need for those people too. Doctors, engineers, lawyers and others were involved in their own professions for their livelihood. In the same way, professionals were required to run radical groups and protests.

But they cannot be considered as daily wagers. Revolutionaries are attracted by a policy and they contribute themselves to enact that particular policy. An amount was given as a gift for their personal needs.

Felix had protests as his life and led a hidden life all throughout. If he came out of his hiding, he was in danger of being captured by Okhrana. Felix who was arrested in 1905 by the Okhrana was released in 1912. Before he could enjoy his freedom he was again caught and imprisoned in Moscow. Felix was imprisoned for five years and was released in February 1917.

Lenin looked at Felix as one of the major heroes of the Russian revolution and held great respect and trust for him. Due to his trust, Lenin decided to appoint Felix as the new leader of the 'Militsiya' group which was formed to protect the new government.

There is unconfirmed information that the rulers did not release him then and Felix escaped from the prison once again. Since there is no sufficient proof to prove this claim, we have to believe that Felix was released in 1917.

After coming out from prison, Felix joined the Bolshevik Party. He declared that he was ready to do everything he could to help the Russian revolution.

It was during that time that the Russian revolution against the Tsars was at its final stage. Felix's experience and skill set were an asset to the Bolshevik group at that time. More than everything, his commitment to the cause attracted everyone toward him. Many revolutionaries admired his dedication in whichever task he started and wanted to follow him.

Within a few weeks ,Felix became popular among the Bolsheviks. While several leaders were praising his dynamic approach and energy, he was introduced to Lenin.

Lenin looked at Felix as one of the major heroes of the Russian revolution and held great respect and trust for him. Due to his trust, Lenin decided to appoint Felix as the new leader of the 'Militsiya' group which was formed to protect the new government.

Although Felix had no significant relationship with the police other than that he was arrested numerous times, Lenin believed that only a person who was named as 'Iron man' and who never failed to complete the tasks which he had undertaken could perform efficiently. Felix understood the trust Lenin had on him and immersed himself completely in his new responsibility.

Felix decided that his first priority was to find the groups which were operating against the Bolshevik group and punished them.. He did not waver from this decision till his end. But, unlike Felix's expectation, Militsiya could not operate with freedom. The reason for that was the internal affairs group which controlled the Militsiya.

Felix was given the responsibility of taking control of several post offices and telegram offices in Russia during the revolution. It was a challenge to maintain the captured offices under their control. Butthe role of Militsiya was not to safeguard the post boxes, but to find protests and riots against the ruling Lenin government and to suppress them.

If that is so, what is the difference between Okhrana and Militsiya?

Okhrana safeguarded the Tsars and Militsiya safeguarded the rulers. Apart from this single difference, both the groups operated similarly. They had similar objectives in finding the opposing members and crushing them altogether.

Although Felix understood the similarity between both the groups, he believed that unless the murmurs against the new government were crushed, a chance to prove the policies of the noble communism to the world would be missed.

The people's rule that was prevailing in Russia was observed by the whole world. Once Lenin and his comrades effectively followed the principles of communism and brought real prosperity to the country, nobody could deny the effectiveness of communism.

But time, opportunity and power to try and prove the benefits of communism had to be provided to the new government.

If they had to spend most of their time in thwarting the local protestors, they could not concentrate on the most important matters.

Moreover, if the government got toppled due to the plots framed by the opposing groups, it would be looked upon as a failure of communism. People would ridicule them as they had claimed communism was the medicine for all socio-economic problems.

Felix decided that his first priority was to find the groups which were operating against the Bolshevik group and punished them.. He did not waver from this decision till his end.

But, unlike Felix's expectation, Militsiya could not operate with freedom. The reason for that was the internal affairs group which controlled the Militsiya. That group was struggling to coordinate Russia and other regions surrounding it into a proper form after the Russian revolution. So, they had several crises including local bodies and the troubles they had. They could not give more importance to Militsiya in their struggle. Even if they were ready to look into it, they did not have enough experience to handle it.

How much could a single person namely Felix do? He lost his cool at some point and wrote a letter to Lenin explaining all the struggles Militsiya faced.

The contents of the letter which was the seed for the sprouting of KGB was: 'The responsibility which you gave me is very important. It is essential for the stability of our government. Such a task cannot be done parttime. So, we need an organisation solely for this purpose.'

Felix's style was always direct. He clearly informed Lenin that Militsiya could not be run as a dummy group and a separate organisation was needed. Lenin understood the truth that was written in the letter. He decided to form a new organisation to spy on those who worked against the government, to control their actions and other similar protection services. That organisation which was started on Felix's request and under his control, governed Russia and Soviet Union for several years as an unmovable political force.

❑

6
Extraordinary

If war, famine or natural calamities occurred unexpectedly in a nation, the situation of the country would change altogether. People might not even get their basic needs. Hoarders would be actively hoarding things. A few might exploit the tension and itch to start new riots and even try to topple the government.

During such situations, extraordinary teams would be formed to handle the situations. The only goal of these extraordinary teams would be to plan and execute activities to handle the extraordinary situations and to come out of it successfully.

We have to note down two words here—temporary and extraordinary.

For example, if a country is suddenly affected by famine and if its people are starving, a ration committee can be formed to supply them with food materials or to distribute cooked food to them.

These committees would be given all the facilities and complete power during the famine period. Only then, they can help others without waiting for others' permission. They can also control those who exploit the situation with an iron grip.

> *When the Tsarist government was overthrown and the Bolshevik government was formed under Lenin's leadership, a few disgruntled men tried to gather public support by conducting demonstrations, rallies and strikes. Although most of the Bolshevik members ignored these protests, they were hesitant to turn their back completely to the protestors.*

But, in such situations, when the famine is gone and when situation returns to normal, these extraordinary committees will not have any need or work, so they will dissolve such committees.

The Cheka, a Russian protective committee formed by Felix in 1917 was initially formed as an extraordinary committee.

What was that extraordinary situation in Russia which necessitated the formation of Cheka?

When the Tsarist government was overthrown and the Bolshevik government was formed under Lenin's leadership, a few disgruntled men tried to gather public support by conducting demonstrations, rallies and strikes. Although most of the Bolshevik members ignored these protests, they were hesitant to turn their back completely to the protestors.

The new government could not assess if the opposing people worked independently or if there was somebody to puppet them from the background. If they had the confirmation that those people were just disgruntled individuals, they could be ignored altogether and the government could carry on with their administration.

But, the Lenin-led government was sceptical if that was the case and whether some foreign power, i.e., if some anticommunism countries were backing them. They had just formed the government and they had not regulated anything, starting from government buildings to their army. In such a situation, what was the guarantee that those foreigners would not start internal riots, cause havoc and when the situation was vulnerable, what if they attacked the country from outside?

> *The full name of Cheka which was formed within a few weeks after the birth of the Bolshevik government was 'All-Russian Extraordinary Commission for Combating Counter-Revolution and Sabotage' which was a committee formed to fight against revolution and damages caused against the Russian government.*

It was not an easy task to monitor and secure the borders of Russia which was huge in both its area and perimeter. Hence, they decided that if the protests were to be ignored then, it might cause invasion from outside through the traitors.

Bolshevik comrades believed that the Western countries which were sunk in capitalism were trying to demolish communism. Hence, they decided that until they got control over the whole Russia, it was dangerous to permit internal revolutions. Although it was an attempt to safeguard their government, we have to appreciate that they did not want to lose the people's government to some capitalists.

Due to various such reasons and the unstable situation which was prevalent in Russia after the revolution, Lenin and his comrades decided that they needed an extraordinary security force similar to Cheka. But, at the same time, they believed that once the initial instability and awkwardness got settled and when the Bolshevik government was stabilised, they would not need a secret police force like Cheka.

The extraordinary nature and its temporary mission can be seen in this group's name 'Cheka' or 'Vecheka'.'.

The full name of Cheka which was formed within a few weeks after the birth of the Bolshevik government was 'All-Russian

Extraordinary Commission for Combating Counter-Revolution and Sabotage' which was a committee formed to fight against revolution and damages caused against the Russian government.

Cheka which has a name similar to a political party was a temporary commission formed to handle the Russian situation after the revolution. The idea to utilise it as a permanent political weapon occurred to the Russian leaders only after many years.

> *Cheka's founder Felix believed that those who worked in Cheka should have a few qualifications and those who developed such qualities to join Cheka should feel proud to be a Chekist. He was the one who emphasized the term 'Chekist' as a symbol of honour. He defined the qualities of Chekists as hard workers, but with soft hearts, unwavering and honest.*

In 1918, Cheka's name was modified a little. They added Profiteering and Official Corruption to its name.

Apart from a few minor changes, Cheka operated in the same pattern with the same goals for almost four years. But, based on the political and social scenes of Russia, the number of its employees and the methods involved evolved gradually.

Cheka was founded on 20th December, 1917. All its members were proudly called Chekists.

Although it was changed to Cheka in 1922, the name 'Chekists' and the pride associated with it did not change. There are many Bolshevik/communist leaders who proudly announce themselves as Chekists even today. One famous example is Vladimir Putin who worked in KGB before becoming the Russian prime minister.

Similarly, the day Cheka was born was celebrated as the Chekists' Day for several years. Due to this reason, the Cheka and the Chekists who worked in the later forms of Cheka did not get their salary of the first on every month. They got their salary on the twentieth when Cheka was founded. They were proud to do so.

Cheka's founder Felix believed that those who worked in Cheka should have a few qualifications and those who developed such qualities to join Cheka should feel proud to be a Chekist. He was the one who emphasized the term 'Chekist' as a symbol of honour. He defined the qualities of Chekists as hard workers, but with soft hearts, unwavering and honest. He defined the qualities and encouraged everybody to follow them.

The same Okhrana which bossed around the revolutionaries under the command of the Tsars. During the revolution, Okhrana spied on almost all the Bolshevik leaders. Since the revolutionaries could not know who was the traitor among them, they were under stress of arrest all the time.

Felix did not stop with promoting his principles, he followed them until his end. Nobody could question his responsibility or his accountability till date. He was one of the major leaders who led Cheka without a glitch. He was a pioneer for those who joined Cheka following him and for the next generation Chekists too. Felix's place in the history of Russian security and intelligence in nowhere lesser than that of Lenin, Stalin and others.

Felix and Lenin both clearly understood the necessity of Cheka when it was formed six weeks after the revolution. But they could not determine its duties precisely then.

Cheka was initially formed as an 'adhoc' commission. Its goal was clear, but a plan was not in place on how to reach it. Yet, they could not wait until a plan was put in place. Hence, they decided to start doing what was important at that point and to develop a full-fledged plan gradually. The authority held by Cheka was also not formulated clearly when it was formed. Cheka found its path only during its course.

Since Felix also did not have a proper training or experience in the field, he had difficulties in deciding how to operate and which method to follow during the initial days. But, when the whole country was under pressure, there was no time to think about formulating a path for Cheka. So, they just started to follow Okhrana's path.

But, which Okhrana?

The same Okhrana which bossed around the revolutionaries under the command of the Tsars. During the revolution, Okhrana spied on almost all the Bolshevik leaders. Since the revolutionaries could not know who was the traitor among them, they were under stress of arrest all the time.

They had to copy the methods of Okhrana who tortured them once, for their own Cheka. Although Felix and others came to this decision due to the lack of other options, there were a few basic reasons for their decision.

But what was Okhrana?

Okhrana was a group to control the revolutionary activities against Tsars which was the governing entity then. When looked through that perspective, there was not much difference between the goals of Okhrana and Cheka.

Opposing parties including Bolshevik were fighting against the government then. Bolshevik became the government later and somebody else was fighting against them. So, Okhrana and Cheka were similar in suppressing the opposing parties.

Although Okhrana operated for more than thirty-five years in Russia, its size was small until its closure. Despite their size, they had a considerable victory in controlling demonstrations and riots to a certain extent.

On the other side, Bolshevik comrades understood it through their experience that in order to reach the same level of success like Okhrana, it would be better for them to follow Okhrana's method.

Several methods followed by Okhrana during the Tsar rule were severely criticised by Bolshevik members. Although they did not want to implement such cruel oppressive measures on the public, they decided to follow the benefits in their enemies' process instead of wasting time thinking about the best way to follow.

Bolshevik members who had experienced the activities of Okhrana at first-hand, the methods they employed to spy on them and the ways their plans were demolished, decided to face their own enemies in the same style.

Cheka did not accept that they followed Okhrana's steps during their initial days even after morphing into several names and stabilising, finally as KGB. They did not want themselves to be compared with Okhrana which was one of the symbols of the Tsar's tyranny.

Cheka did not accept that they followed Okhrana's steps during their initial days even after morphing into several names and stabilising, finally as KGB. They did not want themselves to be compared with Okhrana which was one of the symbols of the Tsar's tyranny.

Moreover, although Cheka started to follow Okhrana's methods during its initial days, it soon formulated a path for itself. The achievements of the Chekists in the intelligence field were way above Okhrana's capability.

Most of the Chekists were given just two tasks in the beginning:

Firstly, finding protests and reactions against Bolshevik government all over Russia and stopping them.Secondly,handing over the accused to a special court named the 'Revolutionary Tribunal', file a case against them and get them suitable punishments for them

Cheka started with these two responsibilities in Petrograd city. but later, when the Soviet government changed its official centre to Moscow, then Cheka also moved to Moscow.

In later years,the yellow building named 'Lubyanka' which was chosen for Cheka in Moscow became famous as the headquarters of KGB . An insurance company was operating in Lubyanka which was built before the Russian revolution in 1898. Chekists evacuated the insurance company and converted the building as their primary office in 1918.

Although the name Chekaits goals, policies, methods, leaders, officers, agents and almost everything changed with time, Lubyanka did not change. When you say the name KGB to a Russian, the yellow Lubyanka building would flash in their mind proudly.

The Chekists did not have the necessity or the time to involve themselves in slow detection. Those who talked against the Bolshevik government, who planned and gathered people for protests, riots and demonstrations, were all over the country. So, the Chekists had to run behind the troublemakers constantly.

Just like Lubyanka, Cheka gave another identity to its grandson, KGB—its emblem.

We have already seen the emblem of Oprichinki which was a pioneer to KGB, Cheka and Okhrana. It was a dog and a broom. The dog was to sniff out the enemies and the broom was to sweep them away.

Cheka's emblem was also designed with a similar thought 'A sword and a shield'. The sword was to fight against the enemies and win over them and the shield was to protect Soviet Russia from enemies KGB took over this famous emblem for themselves later.

Headquarters and emblem done,now what next? Uniform?

The Chekists normally dressed in black long leather coats. Since then, it was unavoidable for all the detective heroes in the Russian movies to not wear a long leather jacket.

What did Chekists detect?

The Chekists did not have the necessity or the time to involve themselves in slow detection. Those who talked against the Bolshevik government, who planned and gathered people for protests, riots and demonstrations, were all over the country. So, the Chekists had to run behind the troublemakers constantly.

Their responsibility did not end in arresting the wrongdoers. They also had to collect evidence against them, submit them in court, answer to their cross enquiries, prove the accused's guilt and send them to prison. It was an uninteresting job, but the authority of Chekists ended with this during the initial days. They did not have any further responsibilities to do.

Despite all the explanations, was it fair for a group which had a sword and shield in its emblem to be so passive and flaccid?

All it took was a few murders and a murder attempt to awaken Cheka.

❑

7
Red Terror

On 30th August 1918, Lenin was invited for a speech to an arms factory in Moscow . Like his every other speech, Lenin mesmerised everybody present there with his captivating speech.

When the meeting was over, Lenin bid farewell to everybody and walked toward his car. When he was about to enter his car, a female voice called him from behind, "Comrade Lenin."

Lenin turned over and saw a woman. Her name was Fanya Efimovna Kaplan.

Before Lenin could ask why she called him, the woman started shooting at him. Before others managed to realise what was happening, she had shot Lenin thrice. The situation was frantic for the next few hours. Lenin was given medical help and Cheka was called for.

Cheka who were aware of those who opposed the government, did not know anything about that woman. They rushed to arrest Fanya and started their investigation. Chekists used all the methods known to them to gather information from Fanya. But none brought them any answer. Whenever she was interrogated ,she repeated the same thing.

"I shot Lenin because iwas planning to kill him for a long time as he has betrayed the revolution and I did it on my own. I will not reveal who supplied me the gun and will not say anything else."

While she was repeating her statements, Lenin survived his attack. Fanya had faulty eyesight, hence her bullets did not reach Lenin's heart. So, he was spared.

The Chekists were unsure if Fanya had personal revenge against Lenin or if somebody had put her up to it. That uncertainty bothered Chekists, yet they could not find the answer. Moreover, Cheka's Petrograd unit's leader, Moisei Solomonovich Uritsky was killed on the same day when Lenin was attacked, by a Leonid Kannegisser.

The Chekists were unsure if Fanya had personal revenge against Lenin or if somebody had put her up to it. That uncertainty bothered Chekists, yet they could not find the answer.

Moreover, Cheka's Petrograd unit's leader, Moisei Solomonovich Uritsky was killed on the same day when Lenin was attacked, by a Leonid Kannegisser.

Cheka was confused if the two events were connected and if the attacks would stop with just two. On one side, a country's prime minister had been shot. There was no progress in the investigation and no suspects were identified. On the other side, one of the major leaders of Cheka had been killed. Cheka was paralysed by both the major incidents.

Before these incidents a few other political murders also happened a few days . Bolshevik leader Volodarski was killed in June 1918. German ambassador Wilhelm Mirbach was killed the next month in Moscow.

Within three months there were four major attacks against the government . Three prominent men were killed in those attacks. Lenin survived out of his luck.

Why was Cheka needed if they could not do anything?

Cheka understood that the above question was on everybody's minds. It also noticed the increase in the count of protests, riots and strikes by disgruntled people. It concluded that an emergency situation was prevailing in the country.

Who gave them the power to award 'instant punishments'? Due to the Russian internal war which started in 1918, protestors, who called themselves 'White Army' gained strength against the Bolshevik government. Due to the prevailing emergency , Cheka was given additional powers to handle the situation.

On 31st August, Cheka started rapid action against the protestors, the very next day after Lenin was attacked. All over the country, people who worked against the government were identified. A few were arrested and many were killed.

On 3rd September, a death sentence was given to Fanya Kaplan for her attempt to murder Lenin. Cheka arrested hundreds of people who were associated with the murder of Uritsky and punished them.

Just like 'savings mela' and 'loan mela' that were held in banks, Cheka ran an 'oppression mela' in the following weeks in Russia. All the trouble makers were found in each area and were imprisoned. Those who resisted their arrests were killed.

But, Cheka's usual behaviour was to arrest the wrongdoers and file cases against them. Who gave them the power to award 'instant punishments'?

Due to the Russian internal war which started in 1918, protestors, who called themselves 'White Army' gained strength against the Bolshevik government. Due to the prevailing emergency , Cheka was given additional powers to handle the situation.

Cheka which was running with twenty three members in 1917, developed into a bigger organisation with more than ten thousand members in 1918. Its growth did not waver again at any time later. In 1986 ,the count of Chekists/KGB employees was 4.9 lakhs in 1973 and it rose to seven lakhs.

In addition to it, on 19th December 1918 ,a special section of Cheka was started . The section integrated the intelligence tasks of Cheka and Russian military together. Mikhail Sergeyevich Kedrov was chosen to be the leader of the newly formed group.

The primary goals of this special group was to infiltrate into the opposing group making use of the chaos created during the internal war, learn their secrets and to counteract their action. Several new and existing agents received special trainings to carry out the mission. They joined the opposing groups in their area, gathered secret information and sent them to Cheka.

With their help, Cheka got information about the attacks of the White Army, their political agendas and prepared counter action accordingly. There was no need to sugar coat Cheka's reaction as a counter action. They wanted the rebels to be terrified of Cheka. So, they punished all the protestors who were captured, in public. The punishments ranged from imprisonment to death sentence. According to the count released by Cheka, Petrograd's new leader Gleb Ivanovich Bokii, on 15th October 1918, around eight hundred protestors were killed and more than six thousand were arrested.

The Cheka reports and news clippings on that period reveal similar information. Hundreds of secret plots against the government were found. Many were killed on treachery claims. Several were arrested. This was repeated in all the reports.

Western historians refer to that period as 'Red Terror'. Concentration camps were introduced in Russia during that period. The concentration camps during Lenin's time were not so cruel as those of Stalin and Hitler. There were also not many camps in Lenin's period.

Due to the internal war, Cheka's importance rose in Russia. It required more agents, spies and officers.

Cheka's punishments started at a lesser level. For example, rations cards were confiscated from those who criticised the government in public. Protestors who were involved in serious opposing activities were arrested. The names of those who evaded arrest were noted down in an enemies list and was displayed in public.

Cheka which was running with twenty three members in 1917, developed into a bigger organisation with more than ten thousand members in 1918. Its growth did not waver again at any time later. In 1986 ,the count of Chekists/KGB employees was 4.9 lakhs in 1973 and it rose to seven lakhs.

Extraordinary Cheka which was formed as a temporary arrangement evolved into an irreplaceable pillar of the Russian government within a short period.

During Cheka's initial operative days, Bolshevik leader Zinovyev once spoke in a Chekist meeting in Petrograd. He declared, "We will not be needing Cheka very soon. We will close all the Cheka offices and will start kindergarten schools for kids in them."

Likewise, another Bolshevik leader Martin Latsis said, "There is no permanent place for Cheka in the Soviet Constitution."

Due to this speeches,the importance of Cheka did not reduce. During 1918 to 1921,Cheka grew rapidly , when the internal war was at full swing.

Cheka's growth was not only limited to the increase in its employee count. Offices were opened in almost all the parts of Russia, arrangements were made to gather intelligence in foreign countries, and advanced training was given. Cheka's evolution was monumental.

Lenin believed that representatives of Western countries raised funds, planned for months and were executing anti-Russian plots in Russian soil. He also believed that such strong plots need strong actions to beat them. There are many controversies regarding the truth of Lenin's belief. A few Western countries might have had the plan to overpower the new communist government in Russia and install their own government in Russia.

The power given to Cheka also increased in that period. Cheka started to file cases against those who were accused to act against the government, gave the verdicts and punished them.

Cheka's punishments started at a lesser level. For example, rations cards were confiscated from those who criticised the government in public. Protestors who were involved in serious opposing activities were arrested. The names of those who evaded arrest were noted down in an enemies list and was displayed in public.

The properties of the protestors who did not stop after all these actions were confiscated or they were banished. Cheka executed softer punishments similar to the above during its initial days. But when the internal war became intensified, these soft punishments did not help them. They had to hand out severe punishments to prevent the wrong doers from repeating their crime again.

Cheka understood it and in 1918, they released an announcement "Traitors, dacoits and conspirators have increased. We are going to give severe and immediate punishments to those who are captured on these grounds. There is no other way for us to control the situation."

This report sent out a warning that Cheka would be taking severe action against Russian enemies.

The report asked for the public's cooperation at its end, "There is no compulsion that only Cheka has to do everything. Russian people should also help us in this regard."

Cheka wanted the public to inform them if they found any government enemies in their area. They also wanted more members of the public to come forward to open a Cheka office in their region. There is no confirmation on how many read Cheka's report or how many came forward to help them. But Cheka had made its stance clear about the actions to be taken by them in the upcoming years.

Cheka's punishments started at a lesser level. For example, rations cards were confiscated from those who criticised the government in public. Protestors who were involved in serious opposing activities were arrested. The names of those who evaded arrest were noted down in an enemies list and was displayed in public.

Cheka started special three-member courts named Troikas during this period to investigate those who acted against the government. After that, arrest, investigation, case, verdict and punishment came under Cheka's control. There is no evidence of anybody asking if a security force should be given all the powers. Even if somebody had asked, they would have been punished.

Lenin believed that representatives of Western countries raised funds, planned for months and were executing anti-Russian plots in Russian soil. He also believed that such strong plots need strong actions to beat them.

There are many controversies regarding the truth of Lenin's belief. A few Western countries might have had the plan to overpower the new communist government in Russia and install their own government in Russia. But there was no evidence to support that the Western countries had joined together to create internal war in Russia.

While considering Russia's economic situation, military strength, weaponry and several other factors, it would not have been tough for all the developed countries combined together to plan and destroy Russia then. Moscow could have been captured easily.

Many says that Lenin's fear and the preventive actions he took were absurd. It can be the truth or absurdity, but Lenin's belief helped Cheka strengthen itself. Since Lenin's government reiterated that obstacles to their people's government had increased and Cheka was needed to manage the situation, the Russians tolerated Cheka.

Cheka accused the British government of trying to overthrow the government and Lockhart and another associate of attempting to assassinate Lenin. It said that a huge disaster had been averted by finding the plan before it was completely formulated.

Cheka released several scorching reports to prove its presence. 'Western spies arrested; plot against Russia was stopped.'

For example, British officer and journalist Sir Robert Bruce Lockhart started to act against the Bolshevik government as a British secret agent. He enabled British intelligence agents to infiltrate into Russia to support him.

While Cheka came to know about this, they planned a secret plot to catch everybody including Lockhart.

According to their plan, a Cheka agent named Eduard Berzin approached Lockhart and expressed interest in his policy. He proudly bragged that he could plan a riot against the government. Lockhart, though initially suspicious of him, was convinced later. Berzin gained Lockhart's complete trust within a few months and relayed their plans to Cheka. Cheka then gradually gathered all the details about Lockhart and his associates and revealed them in public.

Cheka accused the British government of trying to overthrow the government and Lockhart and another associate of attempting to assassinate Lenin. It said that a huge disaster had been averted by finding the plan before it was completely formulated.

It was just the beginning. Cheka revealed more than four hundred plots similar to it in the next one and a half years. Cheka insisted that all these actions are to be considered as a major victory for Russia. The leaders of Cheka argued that both soldiers who meet the enemies directly in the war field and the agents who find the secret plots to diffuse them had to be treated equally.

On 20th December 1920, during Cheka's third annual day celebration, a special wing named INO was formed to handle intelligence tasks outside Soviet's border. The full name of INO was 'Innostranyi Otdel' in Russia which means 'Foreign Intelligence Wing'. Yakov Davydov was the first president of the wing.

At the beginning, Cheka's special section which was formed in 1918 worked on internal problems. But later, it started action in foreign countries too under the name WIB(War Information Bureau).

This Bureau which started in a small way, gradually planted its agents in several countries. Russian citizens living in foreign countries, government officials, illegal immigrants, locals and several others worked as Cheka's intelligence agents.

During the Russian internal war, Cheka utilised the illegal immigrants as their major source of information,the reason was that the immigrants were able to enter into almost all the areas and gather information.

At a certain point, Cheka's foreign intelligence action gained importance similar to its internal actions. So, a separate wing was needed to handle them.

On 20th December 1920, during Cheka's third annual day celebration, a special wing named INO was formed to handle intelligence tasks outside Soviet's border. The full name of INO was 'Innostranyi Otdel' in Russia which means 'Foreign Intelligence Wing'. Yakov Davydov was the first president of the wing.

The initial goals of INO's were:

- Finding and controlling individuals/groups who work against the Soviet government, outside the Soviet border.
- Gathering information about foreigners who enter the Soviet Union to gather intelligence.
- Studying and recording political/economic situation of each country/province.

In certain situations, verdicts and punishments were given not based on the crime done by the individual, but based on the region the person came from, their race or the group they belonged to. Cheka moralised their action that the punishments were not only for individuals but also to the groups.

- Gathering proofs and evidences for all the above.

This group which was formed to ascertain if Western countries really planned to overthrow communist rule during the internal war, was utilised as a political weapon after the war.

We will look into its foreign intelligence activities in upcoming chapters. Let us come back to Cheka.

Cheka reiterated that foreign powers were plotting against Russia during the internal war and intensified its actions, punishments and every other activity. Due to Cheka's actions, several were arrested, punished and killed. Cheka executed the punishments in public to create terror in the hearts of those who planned to oppose the government.

Numerous plots against the Soviet government were unearthed during this period which affected several Russians and a few foreigners. Nobody was sure if all of them were traitors in real, how Chekists confirmed it, whether the investigations were conducted properly or if there were any violations in executing the punishments.

In certain situations, verdicts and punishments were given not based on the crime done by the individual, but based on the region the person came from, their race or the group they belonged to. Cheka moralised their action that the punishments were not only for individuals but also to the groups. So, even if a person had not done any crime, he had an indirect part in the crimes done by his group.

In order to avoid external disturbances ,Cheka started the practice of arresting important persons at midnight. If they suspected anybody of acting against the government or if somebody helped those who acted against the government, they believed that the quiet hours of the night were the right time to arrest them. The reasons were that witnesses would be less and there were less chances of objections or complaints at night.

Suspects that arrested by Cheka were not even given an opportunity to speak out their version of the truth. They were pressurised by continuous interrogations and were made to own the crime. Moreover, they were subjected to several physical torture too. Sensitive people might be traumatised if they know about a few cruel practices the Chekists used on the suspects.

For example, peeling of skin from the prisoners' hands to make 'human gloves', enclosing them naked inside a barrel fitted with needles and rolling the barrel on the ground and many other inhuman torture methods were invented by them. Even innocent suspects admitted to the crime to escape from the torments and got punishments.

The punishment for the traitors or for those who admitted to be traitors was mostly death sentence. If the concerned person had an ounce of luck, they might be given softer punishments like imprisonment or banishment from the country.

There is no official record on the number of people affected by the cruel actions of Cheka during the internal war. An estimate of around two and a half lakh people might have been killed during that period on the grounds of treachery. If this estimate is found to be true, then the count of those who died during direct combat would be lesser than those who were killed on the grounds of plotting against the country.

While Cheka was conducting their violent activities all over Russia, the Soviet public looked upon their actions with contempt. The public started to hate Cheka during the period of internal war.

But Cheka did not reduce their intensity. They retold the same story that several forces were uniting against Russia and the best way to deal with the situation was to fight against them unitedly and to suppress the rebels with an iron fist.

Although there is no confirmation that all of Cheka's activities were done with Lenin's consent, Lenin, who was deeply involved in Cheka's activities during the initial days, did not raise his voice against Cheka's atrocities during the war.

After two and a half years ,when the internal war ended and when the Red Army won Soviet Russia, Lenin commended Cheka. "Cheka acted as an important weapon in fighting against a more powerful enemy and securing the victory."

While Russians and international observers eagerly waited to see if the Soviet government would dissolve Cheka as the war had ended or how the 'extraordinary group' would operate during the peaceful time, a huge famine attacked Russia.

❑

8
Scarcity, Pertinacity

The Soviet Union went through the First World War, the Russian revolution and internal war for six and a half continuous years.

The Russian farmers, workers and public were used to living amid the commotion of bomb blasts. Yet, the dangerous side effects of consecutive wars started to reveal themselves at the end of the internal Russian war. The internal war which started as a fight between Soviet Bolshevik government's Red Army and the White Army who opposed them intensified, and both the parties wanted to overpower the strength of its opponent party.

The Bolshevik leaders had an idea then. What if the government directly bought the grains grown by the farmers in their land?

Although it did not have any direct connection with the war, the Red Army believed that their action would prevent food grains from reaching their opponent, the White Army, and its subordinate groups. Although it might look like a ridiculous plan now.considering the situation of Russia during the war, it would have been a master plan.

It can be said that the government 'snatched' the produce rather than 'bought' them. In many situations, the farmers were not given enough compensation for their produce. Many a time, the army took everything without giving any money to the farmers.

Due to consecutive wars, famine raged all over Russia during that period. Severe scarcity for grains and food items prevailed throughout Russia. It was not easy for the Russians to go to the supermarket and buy whatever they needed just like today. So, the Bolshevik government planned to reduce the availability of food for those who opposed the government. They monitored the farmers directly and bought everything they grew in their farms.

It can be said that the government 'snatched' the produce rather than 'bought' them. In many situations, the farmers were not given enough compensation for their produce. Many a time, the army took everything without giving any money to the farmers.

Although the revolutionaries who opposed the government were affected by this plan,but the common people who had no connection to the war were also affected. But the government failed to consider the plight of the public. They announced that the army had to be given first priority to procure the food items.

But,despite their brilliant idea, the strength of their opponents did not seem to reduce. Although the government fought using the army and Cheka, the White Army grew like mushrooms.

The Red Army analysed how their plans failed and concluded that their opponents were able to get food grains through some secret way. Several farmers were punished on the suspicion that they supplied food materials to the White Army. Numerous farmers were arrested and punished. Cheka increased the severity of their punishments from arresting individuals to farming families altogether.

Lenin's government ordered to confiscate all the extra grains from all the farmers. Due to this order, the farmers lost all their grains which they had stored for their own use and for replanting. All the grains went to the government. This confiscation project was dropped after a certain period. But enough damage was already done. Russia encountered a severe famine which it had never faced any time before.

The famine cannot be described just as a scarcity of food. Agriculture had come to a standstill. People who had enough money with them could not buy any food to cook as there was not anything available to buy. Without any other means, the grains which were kept in stock for sowing were also cooked to pacify hunger. This caused agriculture to come to a standstill and the famine got even bigger.

> *The scarcity was the result of First World War and several social welfare groups helped to overcome it. One such group is ARA(American Relief Administration) which deserves a special mention. It was formed by the efforts of Herbert Hoover that helped to reduce starvation deaths in several countries by distributing food. Starvation is the same, be it a result of a world war or an internal war. ARA came to know about Russia's situation and came forward to help the country.*

The irony was that the government realised that famine has affected several areas, only at a later stage. It could not take any measures at that stage. Not only Russia, but also several other nations were affected by food scarcity at that time. The scarcity was the result of First World War and several social welfare groups helped to overcome it.

One such group is ARA(American Relief Administration) which deserves a special mention. It was formed by the efforts of Herbert Hoover that helped to reduce starvation deaths in several countries by distributing food. Starvation is the same, be it a result of a world war or an internal war. ARA came to know about Russia's situation and came forward to help the country.

The Bolshevik government decided not to let an enemy inside their territory without knowing anything about it. It was true that letting the ARA in the country would have reduced the starvation. But, what if they fed the government's opponents well and turned them against the government?

If it were any other government, they would have welcomed ARA with red carpet. But the Bolshevik government was not ready to trust any of the Western countries. They had a deep suspicion that the group would enter Russia to help them, turn the Russians against their own government and overthrow the communist government.

The people who are starving would consider the ones who feed them as their Almighty; this has happened all through the ages. The Soviet government could not even feed their own people . If a foreign group was able to feed them at that time, wouldn't it prove that the foreigners were considered superior to the local government?

Bolshevik comrades suspected that the American government had secretly planned to overthrow their government through ARA. A few demands made by ARA increased their suspicion.

Firstly,the control of the Russian railway system should be handed over to the ARA.

Secondly, ARA would give food to all the people affected by the famine. The government should not restrict them or ask them not to feed somebody.

Lenin refused to accept the demands of ARA's . He strictly informedARA that he did not need any of their help if they wanted to interfere in Russia's internal affairs.

In 1919, Lenin had no other way in that situation. Cheka's foreign wing was not yet started then. The few existing Cheka agents who operated from outside Russia did not concentrate on the US. So, Cheka did not have the means to know whether ARA was really a social welfare group or if it was a trap.

The Bolshevik government decided not to let an enemy inside their territory without knowing anything about it. It was true that letting the ARA in the country would have reduced the starvation. But, what if they fed the government's opponents well and turned them against the government? The government did not want ARA to feed their people and to turn them against them.

We might wonder whether a government could think like that when the country was slowly facing death by starvation. But the communist government had many such fears which drove them to make several foolish decisions.

Later, when thousands died due to war and hunger in the next two years, the Bolshevik government lost a bit of its pertinacity. On 15th March 1921, Lenin announced a new economic policy. During that period ,the Soviet government allowed foreign groups to enter Russia to help them

Even then Russia's suspicion of the Western countries were not cleared completely. Cheka started to closely monitor the activities of ARA and other welfare groups.

The Soviet government allowed the welfare groups to manage hunger in their country. After letting them inside, Cheka spied on them to see if they were really distributing food or if they were spying on Russia.

Russia's intelligence wing believed that ARA was trying to pull Cheka's employees to their side. Bolshevik rulers were worried that if that happened, it would cause severe problems to the nation's security and to the communist rule's stability.

Due to the severe effects of the famine, Soviet government could not eliminate ARA from their country. But at the same time, they did not change their conclusion that ARA was an arrangement of the United States' intelligence agency. The Americans who came to Russia as a part of ARA and the Russians who helped them were looked on as spies.

Despite all the suspicious looks that fell on them, ARA did a huge favour to Russia at that time. ARA distributed food to crores of Russians. This help continued for two years from August 1921 to July 1923. The Bolshevik government waited until the famine was under control and bid farewell to ARA without even thanking them.

Despite all the suspicious looks that fell on them, ARA did a huge favour to Russia at that time. ARA distributed food to crores of Russians. This help continued for two years from August 1921 to July 1923. The Bolshevik government waited until the famine was under control and bid farewell to ARA without even thanking them.

Cheka had stabilised its internal structure by that time and was running at full strength. When the internal war was at its peak, the public looked at Cheka's suppressing activities against the social groups with contempt. They were scared to raise their voices against Cheka. Hence, they believed that only rogues, scoundrels and sadists would join Cheka.

Felix ,Cheka's leader, did not want to have such a negative image in his group. When he started Cheka, he did not have the intention to torture his own brothers or to oppress them. Cheka had to choose that path in the course of time to meet their needs.

Cheka's actions resulted in severe criticisms against the Bolshevik leader Lenin. He had declared earlier that it was a people's government and everything would happen according to their wish. But they started to torture those who raised their voice against the government later. So, people wondered what was the difference between Lenin's government and the Tsar's rule?

Lenin clearly understood the complaints and questions that arose against Cheka. But, since he believed that to handle all the crises a group like Cheka was needed, he did not come forward to warn Cheka or to reduce its powers.

The Bolshevik government did not like the feud between both the groups. They believed that a gap between Cheka and the justice department would be a disaster to the ruling government and hence wanted to smoothen the rift. The government created an advisory committee in order to support Cheka's actions.

It caused a friction between Cheka and other government departments like the Department of Justice. Also others refused to accept Cheka's superior attitude. For example, the Department of Justice warned against Cheka's independent arrests and punishments. They argued that investigating the crime and to determine the punishment needed was the justice department's responsibility and not Cheka's.

But Cheka refused to accept those argument. They counterargued that the rules might be suited for the common public, but not suited for traitors. They said only when the traitors are given instant punishment, others will think before involving themselves in treachery.

The Bolshevik government did not like the feud between both the groups. They believed that a gap between Cheka and the justice department would be a disaster to the ruling government and hence wanted to smoothen the rift. The government created an advisory committee in order to support Cheka's actions. Several members from various fields including the justice department were made members of that committee.

The mission of the new group was to provide information and suggestions to handle important problems. The government believed that it would reduce Cheka's instant action. Butthe government's belief failed. Cheka did not consult the committee and continued to act on their own and they did not inform the committee about the issues which they had or how they solved them.

A few problems came to the committee's view at times. But even then, Cheka did not follow the committee's suggestions. Cheka believed that all the problems handled by them were important and severe. Only they knew how to handle them and nobody else had the experience or the talent to handle them. So, they refused to accept anybody else's opinion.

The experts and authorities present in the committee were enraged by Cheka's attitude. They quit their position as they did not want to waste time in such place where they were not respected. After dissolving the committee, nobody was able to control Cheka. Moreover, a huge gap was formed between Soviet's important pillars as 'Cheka and others'. This gap could not be bridged anytime later.

The major reason for the gap was the importance given by Lenin and later Stalin to Cheka (and to its other later version).

Whenever a rift happened between Cheka and a government group, Cheka got the direct or indirect support of the rulers always. Although it was blind support, the rulers did not change their behaviour. This made it look like Cheka was more important than any other government groups. This made the others look at Cheka with disdain.

It is not sure if the Bolshevik government understood the scorn others had for Cheka. But a few incidents happened which made the others dislike Cheka even more.

❑

9
Poison Teeth

Felix ,the founder of Cheka's has another name, 'Bolshevik Monk'.

Although he was known for his strictness but was also known for his love toward life, ability to enjoy beauty, experiencing complete happiness in small things and was known as a soft person too.

Felix's philosophies and thoughts have to be mentioned. Several years in prison had sharpened his political principles and educated him to think loudly.

For example, observe this line from his prison journal, 'The melancholy of solitude, a yearning toward something I cannot get, like the air I breathe, like the love needed for life'—he was a person who was capable of thinking like this.

Although he did not have any experience, his confidence and hard work helped him to be an unforgettable leader in the history of the Soviet Union.

During the initial days of Cheka, Felix worked, ate and slept in his office itself, he completely forgot that he had a life other than work. Only two things predominated his thoughts then—to grow Cheka into a strong organisation and to safeguard Soviet Union from internal and external enemies.

> *Lenin doubted the fact that Cheka was needed to safeguard the communist people's government. Lenin observed Cheka's daily activities and provided them with suggestions and comments. Lenin had a major role in Cheka's initial days, giving clever ideas and major decisions.*

Lenin understood Felix's mission and dedication and hence, provided his complete support to him. Lenin doubted the fact that Cheka was needed to safeguard the communist people's government. Lenin observed Cheka's daily activities and provided them with suggestions and comments. Lenin had a major role in Cheka's initial days, giving clever ideas and major decisions.

When the Soviet borders expanded and his job pressure increased over time, Lenin could not observe Cheka like before. Even then, important Cheka documents were sent to Lenin. He read them when he had time and suggested changes and provided his comments.

After that, wherever the Soviet government sent, Cheka was one among the first to set up office in that place. Gradually, Cheka increased the number of branches and was spread out as a perfect network by the end of the internal war. Once it had developed an infrastructure, Cheka took up new missions and responsibilities like:

- Spying upon enemies.
- Identifying enemy spies and diverting them.
- Finding protests, riots against Soviet government and suppressing them (both internally and externally).
- Protecting Soviet Union's border.

- Safeguarding the Bolshevik communist government and its leaders.
- Safeguarding roads, railway tracks, buildings and other national properties.
- Analysing fiction/non-fiction articles in print and other media and censoring them.

Cheka started to utilise its own employees and agents in intelligence activities from then. While compared with the Soviet Union, all other world nations realised the importance of intelligence only later. This led Cheka to infiltrate the Western countries as they had minimum security measures. Their political, science and military information were sent to Russia.

A huge list similar to this was made and Cheka expanded its power and responsibilities beyond its initial limits. The Bolshevik government and the party gave continuous support to its expansion.

Separate wings were created within Cheka to carry out all their actions without any mix-ups. Clear definitions were made on the duties of each member and training; tools and funds were given to them accordingly.

Information gathering wing, administration wing, 'anti-spy' wing to stop enemies, intelligence action and anti-corruption wing were a few of the various wings Cheka had inside it.

Once the task, the member who would carry it out and the method in which it would be done were clearly formulated, Cheka's action took effect with full force.

Cheka started to utilise its own employees and agents in intelligence activities from then. While compared with the Soviet Union, all other world nations realised the importance of intelligence only later. This led Cheka to infiltrate the Western countries as they had minimum security measures. Their political, science and military information were sent to Russia.

Due to intelligence activities, Cheka's importance increased within the government. But, on the other side, people's contempt toward Cheka increased. The reason for people's disdain was that Cheka utilised the extra authority it was given during the internal war even after the end of the war.

Cheka's exaggerated reaction to petty crimes looked ridiculous and there were talks against Cheka throughout Russia.

The price fixed by the government for the food grains was too low and the farmers refused to obey the government order as they would face a loss if they sold the grains at such a lower price. When the farmers' protests started in a few places, Cheka was given the responsibility to handle those who refused to follow the government order.

The Bread War'" which happened at that time buried Cheka's reputation among the public.

We have seen earlier that Cheka and the government together had prevented food grains from reaching their opponents. One of their methods to ensure this was to demand that farmers should sell their grains only to the government.

The price fixed by the government for the food grains was too low and the farmers refused to obey the government order as they would face a loss if they sold the grains at such a lower price. When the farmers' protests started in a few places, Cheka was given the responsibility to handle those who refused to follow the government order.

There was no relation between a security force like Cheka and the purchase of food grains. Yet, Cheka entered the field as they believed that the farmers who refused to follow the government order might turn into rebels and fight against the government.

Cheka monitored the farmers to know how and to whom did the farmers sell their grains. Some farmers were all arrested on the grounds of hoarding food items. That action of Cheka reduced the illegal selling of food grains at a higher rate in the 'black market'. It also reduced the hoarders to a great extent.

Cheka's harsh actions might have been required when the new Soviet Union government was formed and during the internal war. But once the government was stabilised and after the end of the war many commented that there was no use in having a group like Cheka. Many believed that Cheka had outlived its requirement.

But only the merchants could be punished by this action. How to tackle the farmers who refuse to sell their grains to the government?

Cheka concluded that the only way to prevent them from misusing the grains was to confiscate the grains from them. Cheka implemented severe methods to seize the grains from the farmers who failed to sell them to the government and stored them in government repositories.

The farmers were outraged at this and started to protest against both the government and Cheka. Cheka announced that all of them were rich farmers named 'Kulak' and that they were the government's enemies. It implemented the same method used to suppress the revolutionaries against the farmers too.

Due to 'Bread war', small scale farmers, their families, villages, small and large ethnic groups and many others were affected Agriculture was stopped and starvation started to spread in Russia. These were the important reasons for the spread of famine in Russia.

Due to similar activities ,Cheka gained hatred from the public. Many started to discuss if they really wanted such a group for their country.

Cheka's harsh actions might have been required when the new Soviet Union government was formed and during the internal war. But once the government was stabilised and after the end of the war many commented that there was no use in having a group like Cheka. Many believed that Cheka had outlived its requirement. Bolshevik rulers too alleged that the government would get a bad reputation if all the power was accumulated in a single group.

All the anti-Cheka thoughts had reached Felix. He did not blindly support Cheka's actions. He believed that there were a few bad and corrupt men in his group, and the actions of a few of them were causing a bad reputation for the group as a whole. He claimed that there was no need to dissolve Cheka altogether. Instead, he suggested that they find the black sheep within Cheka and to remove them.

He put forth two ideas for it:

- Shoot and kill the Chekists who were involved in corruption and wrong doings.
- Stop death sentence for those who were arrested by Cheka.

There is no clear evidence if the Bolshevik government accepted or rejected Felix's ideas After 1921Cheka's numbers were reduced , . That is, Cheka operated with the same authority as before but with lesser employees and lesser branches.

But Lenin wanted to find a permanent solution for the problem rather than subduing it temporarily. He thought of modifying Cheka to handle only the government affairs and not on the individual problems of the public directly. If Lenin had wanted, he could have permanently closed Cheka at that time. But for some reason, he strongly believed that a group like Cheka was needed to help Soviet Russia.

While analysing the incidents of the previous five years, his belief had a foundation. So, Lenin wanted to pull a few poisonous teeth from the Cheka serpent instead of beating it to death.

On 6th December 1922, Cheka was dissolved officially. To be precise, Cheka peeled off its skin and emerged as a new form!

❑

10
Operation Trust

A new group named 'GPU' with similar missions like Cheka was founded under another special law on the day when Cheka was dissolved.

GPU was also an abbreviation similar to Cheka. Its Russian name was 'Gosudarstvennoe Polittіcheskoe Upravlenie' which meant Russian safety and intelligence organisation.

Although another organisation was started in the place of Cheka, an important change was made by the Russian government to prevent it from being called just a name-changed organisation.

Cheka which ran for more than four years from December 1917 to February 1922 operated under the direct control of the Bolshevik Party and government. But, the newly formed GPU was not like that. GPU operated under an entity named NKVD. NKVD is another abbreviation for the Russian name ' Narodny Komissariat Vnutrennikh Del' which meant 'People's commission for Internal Affairs'.

NKVD already had the responsibility of managing several departments including police, traffic, firefighting, border protection and VIP protection. Managing Cheka's intelligence and anti-government control activities also added to their responsibilities.

NKVD already had the responsibility of managing several departments including police, traffic, firefighting, border protection and VIP protection. Managing Cheka's intelligence and anti-government control activities also added to their responsibilities.

According to the law which dissolved Cheka and formed GPU, below are the primary goals of GPU:

- Controlling anti-government revolutionary activities.
- Identifying and controlling spies who try to infiltrate the Soviet government.
- Safeguarding railway tracks and water resources.
- Monitoring and protecting Soviet borders.
- Stabilising law and order inside the country.

In short, GPU duties were the same as Cheka's. But it was NKVD's responsibility to make sure that GPU's actions did not directly affect the public. In that case, were the additional powers which Cheka had, been reduced?

GPU was given less power as compared to Cheka. For example, they could arrest anybody, but they had to find out within two days whether the arrested person was guilty or innocent and the Innocent people should be released immediately.

What if the person arrested was guilty?

Even then, GPU could not keep them in arrest after two days. Those guilty people should be handed over to the All-Russian Central Executive Committee which was commonly called as' VTsIK'. Hence, GPU was considered as an organisation which had less powers than Cheka in all aspects.

So, the violence in their actions were also considerably reduced in the next few months.

Although the name had been changed from Cheka, its founder was the same Felix. He was the leader for GPU too. Several officers who worked under him in Cheka were in GPU too.

Following the change, all the Cheka branches throughout the country changed their name board to GPU. The officers in those branches continued their job but under the control of NKVD officers.

Following the union, it was decided to merge all the organisations similar to GPU operating in the area under USSR Union into a single 'integrated GPU'. On 15th November 1923, GPU was dissolved and 'OGPU' was formed. The official name for OGPU was 'Joint State Political Directorate'. The 'O' stands for 'Obyedinyonnoye' which means integration in Russian.

Just like the Soviet government's expectations, once Cheka was removed from public vision and GPU occupied its place, the negative comments on Cheka reduced within a few months. GPU focused mostly on non-controversial affairs and it can be termed as the most peaceful period in the history of Cheka/KGB.

In 1922, several communist countries surrounding Russia joined together under Russia's leadership and formed the Union of Soviet Socialist Republics, shortly called as Soviet Union. Following the union, it was decided to merge all the organisations similar to GPU operating in the area under USSR Union into a single 'integrated GPU'.

On 15th November 1923, GPU was dissolved and 'OGPU' was formed. The official name for OGPU was 'Joint State Political Directorate'. The 'O' stands for 'Obyedinyonnoye' which means integration in Russian.

While compared to GPU, OGPU had a superior place in the Soviet rule as a separate commission. That is, they need not

operate under NKVD's control thereafter. Cheka and GPU's leader Felix took charge as the leader of OGPU too.

Another aspect which was made clear through that change was that 'extraordinary' and 'temporary' which were the basics of Cheka no longer applied to OGPU. It was a permanent organisation established under the constitution.

The MUCR (Monarchist Union of Central Russia) was a group which supported monarchy. This group was formed in 1920, years after the end of the Russian revolution. It operated with the sole purpose of bringing back monarchy in Russia.

OGPU, which started to operate with additional powers and new glamour started to strengthen its infrastructure as its first mission. Accordingly, a large number of OGPU branches were opened all over Soviet Union. Several newbies were added as their employees. They were given special training on advanced spying methods and they were utilised both inside and outside Russia.

It was during that period when the OGPU agents (also called Chekists) started to infiltrate foreign countries too. Several intelligence actions were carried out to know what Western countries thought about the new Soviet Union, if they still had the idea of dissolving communism and if yes, what plans were being made.

Almost a year after the OGPU was formed, Chekists obtained news about a new group named MUCR which was formed against the communist rule.

The MUCR (Monarchist Union of Central Russia) was a group which supported monarchy. This group was formed in 1920, years after the end of the Russian revolution. It operated with the sole purpose of bringing back monarchy in Russia.

But, just like several other groups which were formed for similar reasons, MUCR members too could not achieve anything. All such groups lost their power due to the actions taken by Cheka; GPU and later OGPU and others were just running in name only.

So, when the Chekists came to know about the MUCR group, they considered it as one among the several other groups and arrested its important members. But, even after arresting them, OGPU did not leak out the news that they had arrested these people. The reason was that the OGPU Chekists decided to play a game using the name.

The project was named Operation Trust by the Chekists and the important popular spy Sidney Reilly got entangled in the trap and his real name was Solomon Rosenblum. He was born in Russia, but for some reason he hated Russia and his own family and left his country.

Although the Bolshevik government had stabilised in the Soviet Union, there were several rival groups which operated against the government like the MUCR. Despite such groups being investigated and abolished, several new groups mushroomed.

All those groups were small or tiny. But they could not be ignored altogether. If they all united under a common leadership, they might form a significant army against the government. So, each one of them had to be found and eliminated thoroughly.

OGPU decided to use MUCR group as a blanket and wanted to find the other individual groups with a similar mission. But, how was that possible? Wasn't MUCR abolished completely?

Yes, but, only OGPU knew about it. According to the other radical groups, MUCR was still alive as they did not know the updated status.

OGPU utilised the situation and sent a few of its own officers to act as MUCR members. They took their role to their heart, screamed slogans, "Long live the revolution, Bolshevik government, down, down!" and started their spying activities.

It was an accurately made plan. They ran the MUCR group acting against the communist government, obtained information about other organisations which contacted them either directly or indirectly and brought them under their control.

This plan was executed successfully in several foreign countries along with the Soviet Union. In fact, the brilliant intelligence action done by the Chekists in the name of MUCR's ,European wing is still popular among the Russians.

After the Tsarist government was overthrown and the Bolshevik government came to power, Lenin took charge as its leader. Sidney Reilly had to enter Russia then. The tasks given to him then was to analyse how strong Lenin's government was, if they wanted to overthrow Lenin and put in force an England-favouring government, and what was needed to be done.

The project was named Operation Trust by the Chekists and the important popular spy Sidney Reilly got entangled in the trap and his real name was Solomon Rosenblum. He was born in Russia, but for some reason he hated Russia and his own family and left his country. He reached England and joined as an agent in the Britain secret police service. He was given the task of obtaining important information from Russia.

Starting from the Okhrana and Cheka period, Russia was spying on almost all the nations of the world. So, they naturally had the suspicion that other countries might follow similar tricks and gather information in their own land. So, infiltrating Russia and gathering information was not an easy task. Yet, Reilly was attracted to challenges from his childhood and hence he accepted his responsibility with pleasure.

In those days ,Russia was considered an iron fort . Moreover, regular monitoring done by organisations like Okhrana and Cheka strengthened Russia's protective measures. It was considered impossible to get hold of secrets by overcoming all the barriers.

But no one was able to stop Reilly. He followed several interesting tricks and found numerous military, technical and government secrets and sent them to Britain. While the Tsarist government was baffled about the information leaked, Sidney Reilly completed the task allotted to him and went back to England.

Cheka searched for Sidney Reilly throughout Russia. An award of one lakh rubles was announced for those who captured him. But Sidney managed to cross the border using several disguises including those of a Russian farmer, Greek traveller and Turkish merchant.

After the Tsarist government was overthrown and the Bolshevik government came to power, Lenin took charge as its leader. Sidney Reilly had to enter Russia then. The tasks given to him then was to analyse how strong Lenin's government was, if they wanted to overthrow Lenin and put in force an England-favouring government, and what was needed to be done.

Reilly started for Russia in 1918 with these goals. But it was not easy for him to gather information then. The newly-formed Cheka installed several barriers at various levels and protected its secrets with care.

But Sidney Reilly did not lose hope. He thought about how to handle the situation. After a few minutes of thinking, he went to the nearest Cheka office. His plan was not to surrender himself, but to enrol himself in Cheka.

It was the period when numerous newbies were taken into Cheka. Sidney Reilly calculated that if he also joined Cheka along with the other amateurs, he would be able to know all the secrets. In general, nobody can join Cheka easily. Clear information about the interested person and his/her background would be gathered and only after that, a decision would be taken if the person had the qualifications to be a Chekist.

Shrewd Reilly, crossed this step through some means of forgery. He found a spot for himself inside Cheka. He started to utilise his position and gather secrets about the Russian government. He even had the dream of overthrowing the Bolshevik government which was under Lenin's leadership and take charge as the new Russian leader. He was involved in forming a revolutionary group for the purpose.

The situation was like this: a group to suppress the activities against the government, and a foreign spy who managed to become a member of that group and was secretly getting himself ready to start a revolution.

Doesn't it resemble a James Bond movie? There is no wonder in the comparison because Ian Fleming who became popular by writing James Bond stories had admitted that Sidney Reilly's adventures were an inspiration for him to create the character like James Bond.

The only major difference between the real James Bond and reel James Bond was that, although Sidney cleverly discovered several secrets, his dreams to overthrow the Bolshevik government and of becoming the leader did not come true.

The reason was that there was Cheka smelled that a huge conspiracy. Several members who were involved in it were arrested. Sidney Reilly escaped arrest and went into hiding.

Cheka searched for Sidney Reilly throughout Russia. An award of one lakh rubles was announced for those who captured him. But Sidney managed to cross the border using several disguises including those of a Russian farmer, Greek traveller and Turkish merchant.

Sidney Reilly reached London safely and plotted to overthrow Lenin's government from there. Cheka came to know about Reilly's plot and it baited Reilly through its MUCR members in England. Sidney Reilly came to know about the group which wanted to abolish the communist government in Russia through his friends. He immediately contacted the group and expressed interest in it.

Sidney warmly welcomed by MUCR European wing . They all 'planned' to remove Lenin from power. Gradually the Sidney–

MUCR friendship became strong . London MUCR members made minute plans to overthrow Lenin's government and explained them to Sidney without causing any suspicion.

But, how would they overthrow Lenin from London? They had to move to Russia, right?

Reilly hesitated to enter Russia again. He doubted if it would be possible for him to evade OGPU just like the previous time. MUCR boosted him and promised that they would take care of everything. They convinced Sydney Reilly that all other members of MUCR group were in Russia and their confidence would increase on seeing Reilly.

Sidney Reilly succumbed to that age-old trick and agreed to go to Russia. Once he entered the Russian border, OGPU caught him. The official news says that when he entered Russia ,Sidney Reilly was killed in the gunfire that erupted. But, there are several rumours which says that he had escaped and later he was mentally affected.

OGPU used the MUCR disguise to identify and capture several spies, opponents and others like Sidney Reilly. Although Operation Trust operated for several years, they had a high success rate in 1924–25.

Later, in 1927, when the secret about MUCR was revealed to the public, OGPU was considered as the first victory in the history of Russian intelligence.

During the same period, they lost two of their most important leaders.

❑

11
Unfinished Art

The fight during the Russian revolution, the political burden of a new government following the revolution and work pressure affected comrade Lenin's health to a great extent.

Although he survived the attack on his life after taking charge, a bullet which went to his neck moved closer to his backbone and hence the doctors could not remove it. Later, from May 1922, he suffered three consecutive paralytic attacks within a year and was bedridden. After that, Lenin could not involve himself in government affairs. Lenin passed away on 21st January 1924.

Felix worked along with Lenin from their revolutionary days. After the formation of Cheka, they both had equal contribution in strengthening its infrastructure and clearly defining its missions and responsibilities. But, Felix realised that his thoughts, principles and beliefs coincided with another Bolshevik leader, Stalin. So, Felix and Stalin maintained a good friendship even during Lenin's rule.

So, when Stalin took charge as Soviet's leader after Lenin, there were no huge problems in OGPU operating under Stalin. In Stalin's rule , OGPU's importance increased further. Stalin can be called as the first leader who utilised OGPU's protective and intelligence sections as a political weapon. OGPU, which was under the control of a party or a government, started to operate under an individual's opinion after that.

OGPU, which was under the control of a party or a government, started to operate under an individual's opinion after that. Stalin made use of OGPU to manage the political enemies he had in Soviet Union. So, OGPU had an image that it would never hesitate to obey Stalin's order.

Stalin made use of OGPU to manage the political enemies he had in Soviet Union. So, OGPU had an image that it would never hesitate to obey Stalin's order.

There is a popular humour regarding OGPU's obedience.

Once, seven to eight members came to meet Stalin from his native place. They talked about various matters and then left. After they left, Stalin wanted to smoke his pipe. But, when he glanced at his desk, he could not see his pipe. Stalin suspected if any one of his visitors took the pipe and called Felix on the phone. He said, "Comrade, my pipe is missing," and asked him to enquire about it to his visitors who just left his room.

After a few minutes, a paper fell down from Stalin's hands and he bent down to retrieve it. Just then, he saw that his pipe had fallen on the floor.

Stalin immediately wanted to call Felix and inform him that he had found the pipe. Just then, his telephone rang and Felix was on the other end of the line.

"Comrade, we thoroughly interrogated all those who came to visit you. Four of them admitted that they had stolen your pipe and the rest of them died during the investigation," said Felix.

Although it is a cruel humour that OGPU was a puppet in the hands of Stalin during those days.

Felix and Stalin did not operate together for long. Within two years after Lenin's death. On 26th July 1926 Felix succumbed to a heart attack.

Successive deaths of two great leaders of that time affected OGPU severely and modified its path.

Vyacheslav was a Polish-Russian, he worked as a Chekist for a long time and was a disciple of Stalin. These reasons made him OGPU's leader after Felix's death. But, Vyacheslav was not ready to handle such a sensitive job. In fact, he could not do his duties properly.

Unlike Lenin, Stalin started to use OGPU for his personal policies and revenge. The leaders who followed Lenin too did the same and hence, the group which was formed for the welfare of the Soviet Union became a weapon for individuals in the government.

Likewise, Vyacheslav Rudolfovich Menzhinsky who took charge as OGPU's leader could not run it efficiently. This halted the growth of OGPU at its critical time. It enabled the rulers to make OGPU as their personal weapon.

Vyacheslav was a Polish-Russian, he worked as a Chekist for a long time and was a disciple of Stalin. These reasons made him OGPU's leader after Felix's death. But, Vyacheslav was not ready to handle such a sensitive job. In fact, he could not do his duties properly.

The major reason for his indifference was his health. He suffered from angina for many years. Most of the times, he could not even move from his seat. How could a person like him manage the leadership of a group like Cheka?

Moreover, Vyacheslav was not a born leader or a skilled person. One of Bolshevik's prominent leaders, Leon Trotsky who met him before the revolution had described Vyacheslav as an unfinished art copy. Vyacheslav continued to skip his responsibilities after taking charge as OGPU's leader; the reason might be his lack of skills or lack of health.

The history of the Soviet government or police force/ intelligence agencies do not speak much about Vyacheslav due to these reasons. In fact, several associate leaders who worked under Vyacheslav had earned a higher reputation than Vyacheslav.

Vyacheslav did not bother about anything. He delegated most of his field responsibilities to his juniors and did not come out of his Lubyanka office often during his entire tenure.

During the eight years when Vyacheslav was the OGPU leader, several secondary level leaders/officers increased their authority and became prominent OGPU/KGB leaders.

During Stalin's rule, OGPU had to take the responsibility of many government-related duties. OGPU had a major role in implementing a few principle-based actions. For example, the five-year plan started by Stalin in Soviet Union, enabled the rise of several industrial towns.

To build a new house the efforts of hundreds of workers would be required. In that case, the efforts of several hundreds of workers would be needed to construct factories and industrial cities.

Where to find so many workers?

OGPU's contribution toward the five-year plan started there. OGPU started to send its prisoners who were kept in their concentration camps and prisons to work for the creation of industrial cities.

The prisoners worked in all weather conditions, irrespective of snowfall, rain or heat. They were largely employed in all the construction work ranging from digging pits for laying the foundation, constructing walls, laying the ceiling and operating the machines. The Soviet government completed its enormous construction projects without a penny of expenditure by using these prisoners.

But, from where did OGPU get so many prisoners to make them work in such mega projects?

It was a cruel story which both the Soviet Union and OGPU wanted to forget permanently.

❑

12
Weeding Out

Consider you are talking to a friend and walking along the pavement.

Suddenly, two strangers grab you both and each one of them drags each of you in the opposite directions. After dragging you through a small distance, the stranger asks you a question,

"What were you both talking about in the end?"

It is an easy question, but how many can answer in such an agitated state? Wouldn't you forget what you had discussed a few minutes before, completely in the shock of being attacked all of a sudden?

It was the scene Russians regularly saw during Stalin's rule. It was one of the many methods the rulers used to identify the revolutionaries who planned against the government.

The OGPU officers used to separate and enquire innocent public who were seen at a public place together. The same question would be asked to both of them separately, "What did you both discuss together?"

If both the parties gave the same answer, OGPU concluded that they were innocent and released them. But, if any one of them gave a different answer or if they forgot about what they talked earlier, then the OGPU concluded that they were revolutionaries and so they could not answer their questions. Both of them would be arrested and sent to prison then.

There were several tricks and methods followed by OGPU. Their practical nature was ignored and they operated blindly to identify Stalin government's (or Stalin's) enemies. There were a few definitions for the word 'government enemies' during Lenin's rule.

Due to this action, people prepared some readymade answer to give to the OGPU if they were caught. Because, OGPU had the power to arrest anybody on the grounds of plotting against the government.

There were several tricks and methods followed by OGPU. Their practical nature was ignored and they operated blindly to identify Stalin government's (or Stalin's) enemies.

There were a few definitions for the word 'government enemies' during Lenin's rule. For example, people who refused to follow government policies and protested against it, people who gathered men to protest against the government, people who gathered weapons, who tried to attack or kill officers or leaders, 'black market' hoarders, spies, people who sold government secrets to foreigners and so on.

Cheka's major goals was to monitor such people and to stop their actions. But in due course of time, each one gave their own definition to the term 'government enemies' and hence anybody was accused as traitors.

Specifically, the definition for 'traitors' changed daily. At one stage, there was a possibility of arresting every single person in Soviet Union except Stalin and a few of his close associates. The main reason for this ridiculous state of affairs was that Stalin believed that the communist government had several enemies just like Lenin. He announced that there were people who wanted to destroy the government who were present inside the party, inside the country, both inside and outside the border. He said that a few severe actions were required to safeguard the country from their plots.

To enable his paranoia, one of the important leaders involved in the Russian revolution, Sergei Kirov,who was killed in December 1934. An unproven rumour revolves that he was killed by Stalin's people to prove his point. Despite the truth in the rumour, Stalin reaped huge benefits from Sergei's death. He swore to stop a huge plot against the Soviet government and started to weed out his enemies one by one.

The weeding out mission took place under the common name 'purges' and arrested those who thought against the Soviet Union, who acted against the Soviet Union, who planned plots, who helped the opponents and those who were suspected to do all these in future.

The weeding out mission took place under the common name 'purges' and arrested those who thought against the Soviet Union, who acted against the Soviet Union, who planned plots, who helped the opponents and those who were suspected to do all these in future.

For example, right wing members, people who spoke against the communist party's policies, who refused to follow government orders, foreign spies, rich farmers, professionals, educated people, geniuses, public speakers, minorities and several others were affected by the OGPU's actions.

The majority of those who were arrested did not have strong evidence against them. But there was no need for strong evidence too. If somebody posted an anonymous letter saying that a person was a foreign spy, the suspected person would be arrested without any further verification.

They arrested all those who were suspected to be wrong doers. Their justification was what if they were guilty? It was better to be safe than sorry.

Due to these continuous assaults, a tremor of fear ran throughout the Soviet Union. Government officers, experts, scientists, teachers, writers, farmers, traders and others were fearful that they might be arrested anytime for any reason.

People feared that not only the person who cracked a joke or who spoke against the government would be arrested, but also those who listened to them and who accepted their views would be considered as the government's enemies. This compelled them not to talk to others and stay silent within their houses.

People hesitated to talk casually to others. They were scared that they would speak against the government in the flow of speech. They need not even talk against the government, they would be branded as a traitor even if they whispered a joke about the government or Stalin.

In general, jokes might be rated as one ,two , three,four and so on based on the laughter it triggers in the listeners. But, during Stalin's period, jokes against the government was measured in 'two years' or 'five years'.

Two years denoted two years imprisonment for the person who cracked the joke and five years meant five years imprisonment. The punishment ranged from imprisonment till death sentence.

People feared that not only the person who cracked a joke or who spoke against the government would be arrested, but also those who listened to them and who accepted their views would be considered as the government's enemies. This compelled them not to talk to others and stay silent within their houses.

Important people, experts, leaders and others who believed that they might be arrested at any time, kept a ready-to-go pack at their side even if they went to sleep. It contained a spare dress and other personal items they needed in prison. They shivered each time a sound was heard during the night.

Gulag was the abbreviation of 'Glavnoje Upravlenije Lagerej' which meant 'chief administration of the camps' in Russian. It was the government administration which constructed concentration camps throughout Russia and managed them. In course of time, the concentration camps were also called by the name Gulag.

Due to suspicion OGPU arrested hundreds of people and sent them to prisons or concentration camps. It continued its severity in investigating them and granting them verdicts. Based on their suspected crime, the prisoners were physically tortured, threatened and all inhuman treatments were meted out.

The practice of sending all the family members of the accused person including small babies to prison or banishing them from the country was in practice then. So, most of those who were arrested accepted the crime burdened upon them to safeguard their families.

Most of the accused during that period did not have a fair investigation or a formal case filed against them. Even if a few cases were filed, it was not known to the public, the enquiry and punishments were done in secret and the files were closed.

Severe crimes were given death sentence and most of the others received the same punishment. They were sent to concentration camps named Gulag and were tortured to do all the works given to them.

Gulag was the abbreviation of 'Glavnoje Upravlenije Lagerej' which meant 'chief administration of the camps' in Russian. It was the government administration which constructed concentration camps throughout Russia and managed them. In course of time, the concentration camps were also called by the name Gulag.

Gulag was started in 1930 and had separate camps for criminals, scientists and science experts, women and children. Genrikh Grigoryevich Yagoda took charge as Gulag's administrator..

Under Yagoda's management, Gulag morphed from being just a prison where the inmates were locked to human resource centres from which workers were sent to construction and mining works. Scientific experiments were made utilising the scientists and science experts who were imprisoned. Illiterate inmates were used in manual labour.

The number of inmates were a few lakhs who were made to work as slaves in Gulag camps.. There were a few benefits done by them too. Those camps were utilised for building Soviet Union's infrastructure, science and development.

But, the inmates/slaves were not given salary, employment benefits, fixed work timing, recess or safety measures. The Soviet government faced several human rights violation complaints during that time. But the government did not bother about it and the Gulag camps continued to be looked upon as torture camps. People who entered those camps went through severe torture and never came out alive.

OGPU's arrests, death sentences, Gulag camp activities and several other actions created a social depression in Soviet Union. The reasons for it were:

- The stress created by unjustified arrests.
- No opportunity to deny the accusation imposed on a person.
- Compulsory work and severe labour in camps/prisons.
- The prisoners were not even given basic amenities. They had to bear the harsh Russian winter without warm clothes. Many developed serious ailments and several died due to the cold.
- People who were sent to Gulag camps could not see their family.

- Shattered families.
- Untimely deaths.

Thousands of incidents can be listed out like above if we look at all the families which were affected. The Stalin government and its OGPU weapon had terrorised the entire society and made them live under constant fear.

> *The Stalin government and its OGPU weapon had terrorised the entire society and made them live under constant fear. Historian Edward Crankshaw who did research on the Nazis has written that Hitler's Nazi army observed the Soviet's activities of creating extreme panic among the public, making them distrust everybody and utilised them in their country against the Jews.*

Historian Edward Crankshaw who did research on the Nazis has written that Hitler's Nazi army observed the Soviet's activities of creating extreme panic among the public, making them distrust everybody and utilised them in their country against the Jews.

Stalin's successors in the Soviet Union had accepted that their predecessor's activities were not good. KGB had also later taught its agents never to follow such measures and to learn lessons from it.

But all the awakening took place several years later. Stalin who realised that OGPU was a powerful political weapon, did not use it for a good cause during his rule. So, that period and the purge done at Stalin's command remain as black pages in the history of the Soviet Union.

OGPU had a tremendous growth during Stalin's period. Intelligence activities were intensified in Britain, France, Germany and other nations from 1930. Later, it was implemented in the US during the Cold War. Due to their vigilant action, Stalin continued to receive military, scientific and political secrets of all the major countries on time.

But did he make use of all the information wisely?

> *So, the number of opportunists increased in OGPU who guessed what Stalin expected and prepared their reports according to it. Much vital information was filtered out due to it. The rest were changed to suit Stalin's needs.*

The answer is no. Despite the information he received and the sound advice he got, Stalin was known to take instant, emotional decisions.

So, the number of opportunists increased in OGPU who guessed what Stalin expected and prepared their reports according to it. Much vital information was filtered out due to it. The rest were changed to suit Stalin's needs.

The other security wings inside OGPU too wasted most of their time in alleviating Stalin's unwanted insecurities. Party control or rules and regulations were not given importance, OGPU grabbed all those who were considered as a foe by Stalin.

For example, Stalin suspected Trotsky who had equal importance as Stalin in the party and felt that he would become a competition to him in future. So, he started to target Trotsky's followers and arrested them all. Trotsky himself was accused of treachery and was banished from the country.

Following his banishment, Trotsky's followers and friends in the Soviet Union who were collectively known as Trotskyists faced a huge crisis. OGPU targeted them and threatened them to admit that they committed treachery to their country. But they vehemently refused to answer the questions asked by OGPU.

OGPU noted down Trotskyists to be the toughest enemies they had encountered and sent them to Gulag camps. In 1940 ,Trotsky was killed by a Chekist named Ramon Mercader.

There is no official count of those who were 'purged' by the Stalin government. From January 1935 to June 1941, it is believed that around two crore people were arrested and one third of them were killed .

Fifteen members took part in the Bolshevik government formed under Lenin. Stalin was the only leader who survived after the purge period. Many leaders of the communist party were sent to Gulag camps or were killed following a secret enquiry.

Since they had purged lakhs of people, OGPU had made a guidebook on how to capture a person, how to search them, what to do after catching them, how to withhold rumours among the public and several other tips and tricks.

To understand the severity of that period, we can look at a few lines of the 'bravery' song sung by OGPU employees.

"Enemies are clever, but we are cleverer,

Enemies are stronger, but we are stronger,

Soviet people help us,

To pluck the enemies' nails,

To shatter the enemies' teeth,

And to burn them alive in their shacks."

❑

13
Three Leaders

Two important changes were faced by OGPU in the year 1934. The first change was the death of Vyacheslav who took charge as OGPU's leader after Felix's death. Following his death, Yagoda who worked under Vyacheslav took charge as Cheka's (NKVD) new leader.

During that time, the NKVD group which controlled OGPU's previous version, GPU was given additional powers. Once NKVD started to operate with updated powers, OGPU was dissolved and a new organisation named GUGB was formed.

In 1923 ,OGPU came out of NKVD's control. After eleven years it came under the control of the same NKVD but under the name of GUGB.

Similar to GPU and OGPU, GUGB was also a Russian name 'Glavnoe Upravlenie Gosudarstvennoi Bezopasnosti' which meant Soviet protection and intelligence service organisation.

Yagoda took charge as the new leader of NKVD which included GUGB. Following the change, all the individual courts which were operated by OGPU were dissolved. They were denied the rights to investigate the cases and give verdicts all by themselves.

When the public came to know about the changes, they welcomed the effort. They expected NKVD to operate with rightness in their mind. But the reality was that NKVD grew crueller than its predecessor OGPU. Chekists belonging to that group were the ones who did the weeding out mission according to Stalin's orders.

Yagoda , a NKVD's leader was a skilled person of that period, . He had made significant contributions to OGPU's activities especially in running the Gulag camps since the time of Vyacheslav. So, even before the death of Vyacheslav, it was confirmed that he would be the next leader. Since then, all the activities of the group were carried out according to Yagoda's orders.

In 1934, when Yagoda became the leader of NKVD, he made sure not to have any friction with the rulers. He was the one who gave the idea of making use of the inmates and slave employees in various construction work and the one who implemented the idea successfully.

Despite all his achievements, he could not satisfy Stalin in one matter. Stalin believed that Yagoda was not talented enough to suppress the Trotsky supporters. But in truth, several were arrested on the grounds of treachery and were sent to prison during Yagoda's rule. Trotsky's followers were also included in them.

But Stalin was enraged that all those who were arrested were only low-level followers of Trotsky. He thought that Yagoda did not make enough effort to find either Trotsky or his immediate followers. So, in September 1936 ,Yagoda was relieved from the leadership post. As his replacement, Nikolai Ivanovich Yezhov was chosen to lead NKVD.

The next year in April 1937, Yagoda was arrested for several criminal charges. All his followers were gradually removed from their positions and were sent to prison. Investigation for the charges made against Yagoda was conducted in March 1938. The court granted him death sentence for the crime of collaborating with the right wing and the followers of Trotsky.

Yagoda, who was once the fabulous leader of the strongest government group NKVD asked for forgiveness. For his impressive work done by him in forming and managing Gulag camps he requested the court to forgive him . But the court did not accept his request. It gave the final verdict that Yagoda had committed the crime and hence he had to be punished.

Not only Yagoda, but also the authority of Yezhov who took charge as the leader of NKVD after Yagoda also came to an end all of a sudden. Yezhov who was just five feet tall, removed all Yagoda's followers and filled his men in their place as his first task after assuming the office.

But how would the newcomers learn the trade if all the experienced people were removed all of a sudden? So,Yezhov allowed a few of Yagoda's followers to remain and ordered his followers to learn from them as soon as possible.

The newcomers learnt every trick ranging from 'purge' activities to minute intelligence tips from the last few of Yogoda's followers and later, sent them all away or they were killed.

After a few months, all the high-level officers in NKVD and GUGB were only Yezhov's followers. Blood flowed throughout Soviet Union during that period. That period was known as 'Yezhovschina' or 'Yezhov's period' in Russian.

The reason was that the purge activities took place faster than ever before during that period. Around Eleven hundred of the nineteen hundred sixty-six members who took part in the communist party meeting in 1934 were arrested during that period. Most of them did not return from the Gulag camps.

Finally, all the weeding out came to an end. Once a normal situation was restored in the Soviet Union, Stalin started to dislike Yezhov for some reason. Yezhov had not done anything to spite Stalin. Yet, Stalin looked at Yezhov as a reminder of the bloody period. He believed that the public too would consider him as a reminder of the cruel period. So, he decided to appoint somebody else as the leader of NKVD.

Following the decision, Yezhov disappeared one day. NKVD maintained top secrecy in not letting out any news of information about him. If anybody pressed for information, the casual reply was that Yagoda and Yezhov were traitors and criminals.

Just like Yagoda was raised as a successor while Vyacheslav was still the leader, Stalin raised a successor for Yezhov while he was still active. His name was Lavrentiy Pavlovich Beria. He was born in a conservative religious family from the Georgia region. He was attracted by the Marxist policies at a young age and joined the party.

In 1920, Beria joined Cheka and started to gain popularity in GPU, OGPU groups and in Bolshevik Party in Georgia province.

It was during this period, Stalin started to evolve as a great leader in the Soviet Union. Beria was attracted to Stalin from then; the reason might be that Stalin was also from Georgia province.

Beria started to speak supporting Stalin in Bolshevik meetings long before he met Stalin and became his friend. Especially, Beria's emotional speeches supporting Stalin during the Russian revolution were world-known. His speeches were published later in the form of a book.

In 1926 ,when Beria became the OGPU leader of Georgia province, he got the chance to get to know Stalin in person. Within the next few years, Beria became one of the members of Stalin's inner circle and his close associate.

While the purge action took place at full swing throughout the Soviet Union, Beria was the in-charge person in Georgia province. Stalin was impressed by Beria's activities during that period and wanted to give more responsibilities to him.

In 1938 ,Stalin brought Beria to Moscow. The vice president post of NKVD which was under Yezhov's leadership was waiting for Beria in Moscow. It was during that period when Stalin started to develop distrust on Yezhov. Beria understood it and started to extend his influence in both GUGB and NKVD.

Beria became the leader of GUGB within a year after his move to Moscow. Following that, he was appointed as the leader of NKVD after Yezhov.

Once NKVD came under the complete control of Beria, its security division was separated from NKVD and a new organisation named NKGB was formed. The name NKGB meant Public Organisation for State Security and Beria's assistant V N Merkulov became the leader of the organisation.

But the new organisation did not live for long. On June 1941, Germany attacked Soviet Union. Following the attacks, NKGB and NKVD both were merged together. Beria continued as the leader and Merkulov was the co-leader again.

Beria led NKVD efficiently during the Second World War. He was given the responsibility of finding the foreign spies who had infiltrated the Russian Army and to remove them. Intelligence work on other nations were carried out vigorously on the other hand.

The Soviet Union was able to find the secrets of all other nations easily, while other countries could not even peek into the Soviet Union. Many were surprised by their efficiency and applauded the Soviet Union. One among them was Adolf Hitler.

On 17th May 1942 ,Hitler addressed his Nazi army, "We do not have any information about the Russian Army. We could not penetrate their work space. They have severe security and maintain their country as an iron fort. But they manage to get all the information about us through their intelligence work." He commended the Russian intelligence department and saluted them during the meeting.

Beria's contribution had a huge share in all the victories and applauds obtained by the Russian Army during that period. All the awards he won after the war stand as a proof of his achievements.

Beria grew as an important leader in not only NKVD but also in the communist party. In 1939 ,he was chosen as a member of the Politburo and became a full-time member in 1946. Only a few Chekists had got this recognition so far.

While Beria was gradually gaining popularity, the NKVD organisation too faced several changes gradually.

In 1943 an intelligence division named SMERSH was formed from NKVD. SMERSH was founded to investigate if there were any foreign spies inside the Russian Army which took part in the world war. There were a few instances where SMERSH spied upon NKVD officers too. SMERSH sent all the information gathered directly to Stalin and operated efficiently for three years. NKVD's foreign division INO utilised SMERSH effectively.

In 1946, NKVD took a new form under Beria's control. Its name was MGB, Soviet Ministry for National Security. When MGB was created and started to function, there occurred a confusion in the Soviet Union. Another military division named GRU was already there doing similar tasks as MGB.

GRU was formed during Lenin's period and its full name was 'Glavnoje Razvedyvatelnoje Upravlenije'. The name meant Central Intelligence Organisation. It was a senior organisation which was operating along with the Russian Army since 1918.

The Bolshevik government understood the confusion between both the divisions and thought that there would be more benefits if both the groups merged and operated as a single unit rather than as separate groups.

There is another reason for that decision. In July 1947, the US merged all its intelligence agencies and named it CIA—Central Intelligence Agency.

While America had merged all its intelligence agencies, the Russian government thought that it would be a disadvantage to them if their intelligence groups were scattered. So, they merged MGB and GRU and formed a new group named KI.

One of the most important people who brainstormed and formed KI was Vyacheslav Molotov who was the foreign affairs minister of that period. He believed that such a group was essential for collaborating intelligence activities as well as for a few political reasons.

The minister's thought was valid. But it was not easy to implement it in real. The reason was that MGB and GRU both considered each other as competitors and there was always friction between them. Several management errors occurred due to their rubbing against each other. Although several tried to smoothen the waters between MGB and GRU, it did not have any result. So, GRU returned to defence ministry's control in 1948. Their personal feud with MGB remained there forever.

KI continued to operate even after GRU's withdrawal. It was dissolved in 1951.

At the same time, NKVD's leader Beria was unhappy that he had lost his important weapon, the intelligence division. He was expecting the opportunity to merge all the powers as before to be a grand leader.

On 13th January 1953, the communist party's official newspaper 'Pravda' published an enticing news about a plot. It was named a 'doctor's plot' which said that a few Jewish doctors tried to kill important Soviet Union's leaders by administering them poison.

Beria's opponents were boosted by that news. They started to raise a voice that NKVD failed to identify such a major plot made against the Soviet Union. Murmurs arose from several directions asking Beria to resign from his post.

Several rumours started to spread widely before the authenticity of the 'Pravda' news was verified. As usual, the Western countries were blamed for planning the plot. Several rumours stating that the Western countries had planned to kill everybody in the Soviet Union and claim their land floated around.

When the public heard these rumours, they did not bother whether Beria retained his post or not. Their worry was that there should not be another purge planned to manage the sudden calamity.

Another big incident happened before a solution was found for the crisis. On 5th March 1953, a news circulated that Stalin was dead. Following that, Beria, who was Stalin's confidant and one of the prominent communist leaders of that time, took charge as the Vice Prime Minister of Soviet Union.

After taking charge the first task of Beria was to merge MGB and MVD and formed an advanced MVD with him as the leader. MVD meant Soviet External Affairs Ministry in Russian. All the tasks done by all the Russian organisations starting from Cheka till MGB came under the control of MVD.

Beria announced himself as the spearhead of MVD and started to restructure the organisation. He released all the political prisoners from prison. He spoke with emotion and tried to pull people to his side. Other officers and leaders understood Beria's intention clearly. He wanted to portray himself as a great administrator and as a people's leader.

They suspected that Beria was planning to bring power under his control and wanted to check him. Their fear had some grounds. Chekists were powerful enough to terrify the communist government at that time. MVD operated one step higher than the military and all other government sectors.

So, his opponents believed that if Beria wanted, he could easily gather support and take the control of the Soviet Union in his hands as Stalin was also not alive. Since their previous plan, the 'doctor's plot' had failed, they could not reach Beria earlier. So, they planned to make a direct attack on him.

In June 1953 ,Beria's position was relieved from him. He was arrested on the grounds of treachery.Also all his followers were found and were arrested. Beria's authority came to an end in a single day. But the other leaders feared that his arrest might start an uproar and did not reveal it for several days.

The allegations made against him were not minor—criminal activities against the party and Soviet Union, trying to start capitalistic rule in the Soviet Union by joining hands with foreign powers and several others—were strong accusations. Apart from these, there was also a charge of sexual assault against several women.

A special court was formed to investigate Beria. At the end of the investigation, Beria was granted the death sentence for trying to grow MVD into a mightier power than the party, acting independently without following government regulations and operating as a British spy.

Beria was killed. His wife and children were sent to prison. Just like NKVD's former leaders Yagoda and Yezhov, Beria's chapter also ended all of a sudden. For S N Kruglov and all others who took charge as the head of MVD, the history of three great leaders Yagoda, Yezhov and Beria was a lesson.

Government and the party are the most important entities. If somebody tries to develop an organisation stronger than these two entities, they will be suppressed—this was the lesson learnt by the Chekists after losing three leaders.

According to this lesson, MVD was defanged in 1954.

❑

14
Last Name

During his period , Beria accumulated all the powers at MVD. That became his own guillotine.

Once Beria was removed from his position, MVD's power was also reduced. Justice system, internal security, border security, control of concentration camps, highway maintenance and several other responsibilities were removed from MVD.

Finally, the Soviet Union concluded that there was no need for a separate ministry namely MVD. Following that decision, the police force, and law and order was separated from internal and external security.

On 13th March 1954, the security division started and named as KGB. Its full name was 'Komitet Gosudarstvennoy Bezopasnosti' which meant Soviet Protection and Intelligence Service Organisation in Russian.

Cheka which was formed in 1917, took many forms under various names including GPU, OGPU, GUGB, NKGB, MGB, KI, MVD and finally stood as KGB. In 1978, its name was extended to Soviet Union KGB. From then, for about forty years there was no need to change the name.

For this reason, all the groups starting from Cheka until KGB are known by the popular common name KGB. Similarly, all its agents were called as Chekists in general.

When KGB was formed initially, the rulers were only interested in reducing the powers of its previous version MVD. So, KGB had to face severe restrictions from the communist party like never before.

In 1954 ,Ivan Alexandrovich Serov took charge as the first head of KGB. Earlier he was the Vice President of MVD. Although Serov had the black mark of participating in the severe oppression during Stalin's period, he led the action against Beria and hence, he was awarded the leadership position of KGB.

Ivan Alexandrovich Serov was careful not to repeat any of the Beria-period mistakes. Since KGB did not have excess power during that time, no major crisis occurred.

The first problem faced by Ivan Alexandrovich Serov was the Hungarian revolution during October–November 1956. Thousands of revolutionaries gathered against the Soviet government in Hungary. KGB's help was needed in controlling them.

Ivan Alexandrovich Serov himself went to Hungary, planned well and executed the operation against the revolutionaries. The Hungarian revolution was suppressed. But, the severity of the oppression made by Soviet Union on Hungarian revolutionaries shook the world.

Although the revolutionaries worked against the government, the way the communist government which called itself as 'people's government' treated its own citizens was frowned upon by the world. That black mark fell upon KGB too.

In truth, the rulers who came in after Stalin had reduced their violent activities to a great extent. Their behaviour toward opponents were changed. Feedback from the opposition was welcomed and signs of democracy started to show themselves. As a sign of the change, several prisoners were released from the Gulag camps.

Yet, during the peak of the Cold War between the US and the Soviet Union, even small altercations in the Soviet were blown into huge issues by the Western journalists. So, KGB continued to receive negative focus upon them.

In 1958 ,Alexander Shelepin took charge as the new leader of KGB. According to the president, 'Nikita Khrushchev', Shelepin was the one who made significant changes in KGB's responsibilities, infrastructure and methods.

According to KGB, the two most important changes done by Khrushchev was to stop several severe actions of Stalin's period and to frankly admit that they did wrong in a few matters. Khrushchev did not stop with apologising for the mistakes, but wanted to permanently stop such cruel actions to emerge again. Arrangements were made to ensure it.

When Shelepin took charge as the leader, numerous officers belonging to Stalin's period were removed. Active youngsters were chosen for important positions and KGB was revived with young blood. Shelepin proudly declared that KGB was true to the communist party and to the Soviet people. He gradually gained importance in the party through his reformations.

A few years later, Shelepin was removed and Vladimir Semichastny was chosen as the new leader of KGB in 1961. Vladimir Semichastny understood that KGB had a negative image in both Soviet and foreign media during that time. He started to do everything possible to break the negative image and to create a good image of the KGB.

Vladimir Semichastny gave detailed information about KGB missions and the interesting challenges it had to the media and published them as well. This increased the number of Soviet youngsters who wanted to join KGB. At the same time, Vladimir Semichastny tried to ensure the fact that there might have been a few Chekists who violated the public before (during Stalin's period), but they were no longer in KGB.

While he gradually built a positive image of KGB, Soviet's president, Nikita Khrushchev was overthrown from power. Following that, all the reformations were also thrown to dust. The Soviet Union was caught up in oppression fever like before.

KGB's former and current officers had a major part in Khrushchev's dethronement. 'Leonid Brezhnev' was chosen as the new president of the Soviet Union and KGB kept Khrushchev under similar scrutiny.

After Leonid Brezhnev took charge ,KGB started to concentrate on attacking the government enemies either directly or indirectly. Several methods including arresting the revolutionaries, creating fake documents, spreading false news about the leaders of radical groups and several others were followed.

Anti-government talks or misunderstandings were never allowed again in Soviet Union until Mikhail Gorbachev's rule in the 80s.

After the fall of Khrushchev, in 1967 ,Yuri Vladimirovich Andropov became the leader of KGB. He was the only leader of KGB who served the longest period of fifteen years.

Those fifteen years are significant in the history of KGB. KGB which was shrunk from being a ministry to an ordinary government commission during the fifties, gained importance gradually during that period.

To which extent? To the extent of a KGB leader becoming the president of the Soviet Union.

In 1982, Yuri Andropov quit from the leadership of KGB and took charge as the president of the Soviet Union. He was the first Chekist to get that honour. Andropov served in several government posts before becoming the leader of KGB. He served as the ambassador in Hungary when the revolution took place in 1956. He was the major reason for the Soviet Union in successfully suppressing the revolution.

Andropov grew in the party and the communist government through such prominent actions. But when he was appointed as the leader of KGB, several people were surprised. What was his relation to the KGB? Several wondered what could he do in KGB.

But KGB was modernised only during the period of Andropov. KGB which was dependent only on human power to spy upon, started to use electronic gadgets and satellites during his period.

At the same time, Andropov took severe actions against the government enemies. KGB became the world's number 1 intelligence agency by both spying on foreign lands and finding internal wrong doers.

But KGB did not gain any respect in its own land. Most of the Russians looked on KGB with fear. Since they belief that whatever they say or do would be relayed to KGB was deeply rooted in their brains and suspected everybody to be KGB agents.

True to their belief, there were KGB agents everywhere from government offices till military divisions. Everybody's actions starting from friendly banter to foreigners in Soviet soil were monitored.

KGB started to create best spy network throughout the world and started to know the secrets of other countries during Andropov's period.

People who know others' secrets always have the fear if their secrets would also be revealed. The Soviet Union was no exception to it. KGB which had the best spy network in the world was careful in not letting any information theft happen in its own land.

KGB agents followed all the foreigners who stayed in the Soviet Union. If any of the locals became close to the foreigners, they were branded as spies.

In all the application forms of Russia ranging from school admissions, office promotion or foreign visas, a question would be present without fail, 'Do you have any friends/relatives from foreign countries?' If their answer was 'yes' to that field, the application would be rejected for sure. Russians with foreign contacts were troubled by this.

During that period, Soviet President 'Leonid Brezhnev' and KGB leader Yuri Andropov worked together with similar goals in their minds. The influence of KGB members and leaders started to spread inside the communist party too.

In 1982 ,when Brezhnev died, 'Yuri Andropov' was chosen as the new president. In 1988, Vladimir Alexandrovich Kryuchkov became the leader of KGB. Kryuchkov was also a communist VIP similar to Andropov. In 1967 ,he joined the KGB gradually became its vice president and president in 1982. He was one among those who chopped the Soviet Union into small pieces in 1991.

❑

15
Surveillance and Subversion

Other countries of the world did not fear or dread the KGB which constantly changed names starting from Cheka.

The reason was the image of the Soviet Union was a communist confederation who liked to live peacefully among themselves and who do not intend to harm others. Although that was true to an extent, the Soviet Union spied on the whole world to make sure that nobody intended to harm them.

They found it easy to infiltrate other countries in the beginning. They built a strong spy network before the intelligence division of other countries were alerted. The spies who were sent both officially and unofficially to other countries gathered information about the political, military, scientific information, data about their internal problems, important documents, pictures, maps and sent them all to Moscow regularly.

The foreign countries realized the leak at one point and were alerted. They started to look at all the Russians who entered their country with suspicion. But KGB agents had excellent training and were never frazzled by the scrutiny.

The way KGB chose their agents and the training given to them were kept top-secret. The agents were given secret challenges and their backgrounds were thoroughly verified before being recruited. Extensive training was given to all those who were chosen.

They were told the hair-raising adventures of former KGB agents and spies. Although they were given excellent salary and other benefits, KGB trainers believed that the agents should be won over by the policy and not by the monetary benefits.

Field specific trainings were given to the agents according to their field they would be assigned to. The below list is the examples of the training:

- ♦ Training for the agents who would involve in attack and other direct actions.
- ♦ Training for secret agents (local/international).
- ♦ Training to spread false information among the enemy groups.
- ♦ Training to stalk individuals.
- ♦ Observing skills training.
- ♦ Training to operate under the disguise of a reporter.

Secret manuals were made for all the trainings. Each KGB agent was made by following the manual as their life's principles.

The next action plan was to prepare a cover story for the KGB agents in the country or place where they would be sent to. All the documents to support their story would be createdand only after that the agents would be sent on their journey.

In short, KGB never sent any half-baked person into a mission or never sent any agent into a half-planned mission. This made KGB a step above all the other intelligence agencies of the world. Those intelligence agencies made several efforts to find if any KGB agents could be found entering or leaving their countries, but they never identified the KGB agents sitting right under their nose.

There was no single country which they could not infiltrate during the peak period of KGB. The 'Mitrokhin archive' which was released by the end of the 90s prove this point.

When Mitrokhin whom we met in the first chapter, brought out the secrets of the agency by copying them, amidst several complications, several countries were ashamed of their naivety. More than the embarrassment that they had lost their secret information, they were astounded by how the KGB agents had infiltrated them and lived among them as their own.

For example, when the Mitrokhin archive came out, a eighty seven old grandmother named Melita Norwood was known to be a spy in Britain. Nobody can imagine the woman who grew apples in her back yard and sold jam as a spy

But she worked in a company which researched on nuclear bombs in Britain. She regularly stealing information about her company and sent them to Moscow. When the Mitrokhin archive was released, she admitted it openly.

Likewise, the United States' nuclear bomb also did not escape KGB's eagle eyes. The Soviet Union received instant information about all the research made by the US on its first uranium/plutonium bombs through its agents who were sent after perfect planning.

They were able to go ahead with their nuclear bomb production and to quicken its pace. Soviet's bomb blasted in 1949, just four years after the United States' first bomb blast in 1945. They could not have achieved that if not for their intelligence wing.

KGB's intelligence action brought good results in scientific sectors. But their skill was not enough in military and political divisions. KGB received countless information which no other intelligence agency in the world could dream of. But they did not have the skillset needed to analyse the information and to take suitable decisions.

Moreover, Chekists had the mentality that their job was just to give what the leader wanted and nothing else mattered to them.

Most of them had the fear that they might be punished if they conveyed unpleasant information to the leader. So, most of the critical information did not reach their leaders.

Although there were a few complaints like these, nobody could deny the unbelievable achievements made by KGB agents. In most of the situations, the Soviet Union had information about what their neighbours, their enemies and competitors thought about and what they planned to do next, beforehand.

The Mitrokhin archives reveal several examples for this. KGB agents had infiltrated into the higher levels of the United States' two most important security agencies, FBI and CIA. The five-member army from England's Cambridge University poured in several secrets. KGB had penetrated West Germany. It had penetrated India during Indira Gandhi's rule. The Mitrokhin archives revealed many such shocking information.

When the Mitrokhin archive was released after compilation by Christopher Andrew of the Cambridge University, the whole world was shocked. Everybody talked about the extraordinary intelligence agency. The information which Mitrokhin had managed to copy was released as two giant books. All were stunned to realise that many more documents were already hidden or destroyed by KGB.

Many countries including India have a difference of opinion on whether to believe everything mentioned in the Mitrokhin archives. Yet, those books are proof to show how far KGB's foreign intelligence activities were successful.

KGB was proud of their secret activities and strongly believed that no information about them would be ever leaked out. But their bad luck was that Mitrokhin who had the opportunity to read everything wanted to copy them.

If the Soviet Union had not split and scattered in 1991, Mitrokhin's archive might not have been released at all. Mitrokhin moved to Britain after the split. All his secret notes which were filled in six huge boxes were smuggled out of Russia by British intelligence agents.

Only when Mitrokhin's archives were released in two parts, were world nations able to know about the KGB which was a huge black box until then. This made Mitrokhin's archive a historical document.

The biggest commendation for this effort of a single person came from US security force FBI. "It is the most detailed and wholesome intelligence notes ever available in history."

What did Mitrokhin record for twelve years without taking any break? On peeking at it, adventurous stories (or reality) spread before our eyes which would put any crime or thriller novel to shame!

❑

16
World in One's Palm

When we observe the Soviet Union's political situation closely, we can see that although the name of KGB, its leaders, and political process were changed constantly within seventy five years, its foreign process did not waver from its path.

The major reason for it was that since Cheka's INO division started, most of its handpicked best agents concentrated more on intelligence activities only in the foreign countries.

KGB had authority within the Soviet Union. They could use their might to know about secrets which they could not get it through any other measures. But they could not do the same in a foreign country. So, they depended solely on talented spies in foreign countries.

KGB sent all its best spies to foreign countries. Based on their age and experience, two kinds of responsibilities were given to them.

1. Finding foreign secrets and actions against the Soviet Union.
2. Buying officers in rank and converting them into Soviet spies.

The Soviet spy network spread to each country on the world map through this technique. All they had to do was to find a talented individual, create a cover story for him and send him to a country. Everything else would be taken care of by that talented spy.

KGB's plan succeeded in almost all the countries. At a certain stage, the KGB struggled to properly compile the mountains of information it received from all over the world. What the Soviet rulers did with so much information is another tragedy. But the truth was that KGB was able to gather almost all the secret information of all the countries of the world.

Although the information about the foreign agents who were involved in intelligence activities for the Soviet Union were kept as secret, several interesting stories and adventures about them floated around using their code names. KGB believed that by celebrating best agents by portraying as popular characters, they could attract more youngsters into KGB.

For example, a Soviet spy group named 'Cambridge Five' was formed in British soil and brought several secrets to the the Soviet Union. The group consisted of five members and none of them from the Soviet Union. But they have an important place in the chronicles of KGB's spy history.

What was the need for those five youngsters from Britain to be loyal to the Soviet Union?

There proves the ingenuity of KGB. KGB sent Arnold Deutsch to form a spy force in England. The responsibility given to him was to find new agents. It might be easy for Arnold to migrate to England and find a job.

But, what next? How could he infiltrate British government offices? How to find important secrets?

Arnold understood the practical difficulties involved in his mission and decided to follow a different approach. His plan was simple. It was difficult or time-consuming for a KGB agent to access British secrets. What if they turn a few who could access British secrets into KGB agents?

Although it sounds simple, but implementing the plan was complicated and dangerous too. People who knew about British political, military and scientific secrets which Arnold and KGB needed were only a few. Arnold could not call them directly and ask for the secrets.

Although it was true that buying a few officers who knew the information was practical, how could they find who could be bought and who could not? What if they let out their identity to a wrong person who was loyal to Britain? Wouldn't it be a huge embarrassment to Arnold and to the whole of KGB?

Arnold thought about it and proposed a plan. "Let the existing government officers be as they like, let us find future government officers"

What did he mean by future government officers?

A Tamil movie named *Ramana* was released a few years ago. Its leading character was a college professor who made an excellent plan to stop corruption in government offices. He chose a few of his best students and changed them into honest human beings. Later, he prepared them to become government officers and sent them to work in various government offices through Tamil Nadu.

That method chosen by professor Ramana to spread honesty was popular and was made into movies in several languages. Magazines and other media raised an important question when the movie was released. "Will this work in real life?"

Real life can be more bizarre than fiction at times. Arnold Deutsch could be said as the pioneer to the fictional professor in *Ramana.* Arnold, who was operating with the intention of creating a KGB spy force in England, found a few students of British Universities and developed friendship with them. Gradually, he changed them into followers of communism.

As the next step of his plan, all the students were prepared for government jobs. KGB got a strong spy infrastructure in British government offices through them. There could not be an easier or more practical plan than that.

Wasn't it clever to turn talented students into spies rather than approach existing government officers and get into trouble?

For his plans, Arnold chose two universities—Oxford and Cambridge. He observed that out of the two universities, more students from Cambridge were able to crack government jobs.

Moreover, he found his first agent from Trinity College belonging to Cambridge University. His name was Kim Philby. Kim Philby developed communist thoughts even before meeting Arnold. When he was working in Vienna, his wife Litzi's friend Edith observed him closely. She concluded that he could be changed into a Russian spy with minimum efforts.

Kim and Litzi soon returned to London. Edith had already migrated to London and arranged for a meeting between Arnold and Kim. After a single meeting with Arnold, Kim became a loyal spy to the Soviet Union.

Arnold did not even mention that he was a KGB member or his expectation of Kim to operate as a Soviet spy. He just asked Kim to help communism to fight against capitalism. But that simple request was enough for Kim. He surrendered himself completely and was ready to do anything.

The first task given to Kim by Arnold was to cut all his ties with his communist friends, not to talk, write or act in favour of communism and never to reveal himself as a supporter of communism. Kim was not taken aback by the instruction. He understood that the first task of a spy was to disguise his real identity and to act like somebody else. If British officers suspected Kim of being a communist, they would not have allowed Kim inside their network despite his talents.

Next, Arnold asked Kim about his friends who might want to join their team. He was able to find like-minded active youngsters through Kim. There were five members who were chosen by Arnold including Kim. All were alumni of colleges of the Cambridge University. All five of them wanted to become spies of communist Soviet Union not for the money or name but for its principle.

- Kim Philby
- Anthony Blunt
- Guy Burgess
- John Cairncross
- Donald Mclean

Once these five members who were known as the 'Cambridge Five' entered England's government and related organisations, they started tosteal secret information to Moscow. KGB received instant updates about everything including England's political status, military activities and important scientific inventions.

Kim Philby got a job in a British intelligence agency. So, he was able to gather information on international affairs about US and other countries from his place. But the information gathered by them could not be sent directly to Moscow. Arnold's master brain worked on that.

Arnold was careful in not letting anybody cast their suspicion on those five who were in important government positions. So, he followed several secret manoeuvres to gather information from them.

If Arnold wanted to meet one of the agents who had the microfilm copies of sensitive or secret information, he would drive to the outskirts in his car. That precaution was to observe if anybody followed him.

After roaming around for some time, after shaking off any one following him, he stopped his car at some place and boarded a public bus all of a sudden. After travelling in bus for some distance, he got down and boarded another bus or a train. After shifting to some other public transport, he would finally reach

London. If anybody had followed him, they would have lost him by then.

Arnold operated carefully without leaving any space for even a small mistake. He was a talented and learned man, and More than anything else, he knew how to handle people by gaining their complete trust.

Arnold spoke to anybody with complete concentration and kindness which made the listener feel that he was the most important person in the whole world. Kim Philby had mentioned that he could sense that Arnold was a great person even during their first meeting and that opinion had never changed.

While the intelligence activities of the Cambridge Five under Arnold's supervision were successfully functioning, they got a double benefit through an incident. Kim Philby was given the responsibility to handle all the British intelligence tasks concerning Russia. Through this assignment, Kim's work of sending England's secrets to Russia became easier. At the same time, he was able to hide or filter the information sent to England by the British spies in Russia.

Kim Philby operated efficiently by being doubly loyal to the Soviet Union and without attracting any suspicion on himself. Several important responsibilities and honorary posts came to him for his efficiency. If anybody had told the England officers that Kim was a Soviet spy, they would have laughed out aloud. Kim Philby carried out his 'duties' with great precision and without any hesitation.

At that time, Britain sent Kim Philby to the US with a significant responsibility. His spying brain did not stay still in the US too. He gathered vital information about the United States' nuclear weapon research and sent them to the Soviet Union. Unlike Britain, US found the leak easily. When they investigated the root cause of the leak, Kim and his friends' names were uttered.

Following that, two of Kim's friends escaped to Russia to evade arrests. Kim was charged on tipping off his friends and was taken to London. No useful information was obtained during the investigation British government made on Kim. Since none of the crimes alleged upon him had valid evidence, he was asked to submit his resignation and was let go.

Kim Philby worked as a reporter for some time. When he faced a problem in his job, he fled to Moscow and joined KGB officially. Important responsibilities and major positions waited for him in KGB.

Although the era of 'Cambridge Five' ended soon, KGB's action inside Britain did not stop with that. Until the release of the Mitrokhin archive, nobody knew that KGB had securely hidden several other spies in Britain.

Skilled KGB agents infiltrated almost all world nations besides England. Superpower US was also not exempted from it. Even before the Soviet Union confederation was officially formed, agents belonging to Cheka/GPU and Russian Army's GRU group started to infiltrate several countries. But they did not consider the US as a huge threat then.

When the Soviet Union decided to enhance their intelligence activities, the three major countries which they considered were England, France and Germany.

Not only the Soviet Union, most of the world countries did not consider US as their enemy in those days. Nobody was interested to know what happened inside the US. So, while compared to the other countries, KGB agents who operated within the US during the early 30s were less.

But, those 'lesser' members were enough for the US to frown upon KGB. The US warned KGB that they do not like them interfering in their affairs. In 1933 ,the treaty signed by the US and USSR, it was mentioned as a major concern. But, just like America's distrust, the count of Russian spies in the US did not reduce even after signing the treaty. In fact, the count of direct and indirect spies increased after the treaty.

The same formula which worked in other countries was followed in the US too. Russians who were living in the US, big shots who were buyable with money and communist supporters were found and were converted into Russian spies. Within no time, a perfect KGB spy network was formed in the US too. The US was flabbergasted at not being able to find who were the KGB spies and who operated directly or indirectly.

Their chief suspicion was of the Communist Party of the US (CPUSA). The US suspected that its general secretary, Earl Browder and a few of his followers were indirectly gathering people to work as Soviet spies. They were able to confirm their suspicion only after half a century.

Jacob Golos was one of the most important Soviet spies who worked in the US during that period. He was one of the senior officers in the Communist Party of the US. He proudly declared himself as a Chekist. His continuous efforts enabled several KGB agents to work freely without any constraints in the US.

Jacob Golos had started a tourist service agency named 'World Tourists'. His agency was the reason behind several Soviet spies entering the US either under their own name or in disguise.

Several countries were worried as to how the US would contribute and which nation would it support during the Second World War. Those countries were scared that it would be a huge problem for them if the US made a move against them. So, they activated their own intelligence division to know about the United States' political situation, military strength, scientific discoveries and to control them.

Jacob Golos operated efficiently during that period, found several talented people and added them to his spy network. The spy network which he formed was later called as 'Golos Ring'.

The first victory of KGB (i.e., its previous version GPU/ NKVD) in US soil was the murder of Bolshevik leader Trotsky who fought against Stalin's rule. Trotsky who was banished from the Soviet Union in 1929, hid himself in Turkey, France and Norway for some time. Finally, he reached Mexico.

Trotsky's books and his political actions during his hidden life irritated Stalin. He decided to silence him and made arrangements for it. In May 1940, a GPU team under the leadership of agent Iosif Romualdovich Grigulevich forcefully entered Trotsky's house. But luckily, Trotsky escaped from their grasp.

Following his escape, a small change was made in the plan. Instead of attacking him as a group, they decided to let a single KGB agent become close to Trotsky and gain his trust. Once that was achieved, they decided to fulfill their mission. A NKVD spy name Ramon Mercader did not participate in the earlier attack was chosen for the mission.. He entered Mexico under false identity and started to spy on Trotsky's circle of close friends.

He announced himself as Trotsky's fan and informed that he was from Canada. Nobody doubted him and hence he had the opportunity to meet Trotsky often and to talk to him. Within three months after the initial attacks, Mercader went to meet Trotsky on 20th August and utilised the opportunity to kill him with a pickaxe.

Although Ramon Mercader was caught red-handed after Trotsky murder, this incident was a proof to KGB's fool-proof plan even outside the Soviet Union. Western countries' media started to observe KGB with caution after that.

Another task given to the KGB agents in US during that time was to gather information about nuclear weapon research. A special division named XY Cell was made solely for that purpose.

Russian scientists were significantly developed in scientific research and they could have invented a nuclear weapon without bothering about the US. But it might have taken more time and there was no guarantee that the US would be patient until Russia found their nuclear weapon.

Due to that fear, the Soviet Union wanted to know everything about the United States' nuclear weapons. The Soviet Union was ready to make a carbon copy of their nuclear bomb and strengthen themselves.

The XK Cell formed for this purpose was handed over to Jacob Golos. He found engineers, scientists and others who had an adherence to the Soviet Union and communism and made a team. That team operated under the leadership of Julius Rosenberg and sent several vital information to the Soviet Union through Golos.

In addition to him, several agents including Theodore Hall and Klaus Fuchs gathered information about nuclear weapon research which was called 'Project Manhattan'. The information and secret notes gathered by them quickened the Soviet Union's nuclear weapon manufacturing speed. As a proof of the Soviet Union's invasion inside the US, Soviet Union manufactured and blasted a nuclear bomb in 1949 just four years after US blasted their first bomb in 1945.

After witnessing it, the United States' suspicions were confirmed. KGB had infiltrated US and all other countries like no other agency in the history of intelligence. US decided to control KGB through any possible way during the Cold War period between the US and Soviet Union. US tried to safeguard its secrets through several protection measures. But KGB struggled to operate freely as before, inside the US.

Thus, KGB's intelligence activities continued despite severe restrictions. Until Soviet Union shattered into pieces in 1991, there was no lack of news about KGB agents inside the US.

Despite the number of times they were crushed, KGB marched on with renewed strength and it was their major asset. KGB agents were ever-present in the US, Europe, Asia and everywhere. The countries might not even realise KGB's presence. But KGB gathered information from all the countries without classifying them as a small or big country.

For example, India had a good relationship with Soviet Union. Yet, Mitrokhin archives revealed that KGB's spying hands had penetrated deep and wide in India. In fact, Mitrokhin said that India was one among the countries where KGB was able to infiltrate both easily and completely.

Especially, it looks like several government officers, leaders, politicians and others received incentives from KGB and showered them with all the information during Indira Gandhi's rule. So, there were not many adventures in India while compared to US or Britain. But India became one of the biggest KGB networks that was weaved outside the Soviet Union.

Likewise, KGB agents infiltrated the Indian embassy in Moscow right from Indian independence. KGB had bought several Indian officers who were in chief positions and knew all the information that went to and from India.

India sent all their official information hidden through cryptology with or without knowledge about KGB's eavesdropping. So, KGB could not understand the content sent in the messages. That is, they had access to all the important documents or its copies easily. But they could not understand what was written in it. KGB thought about decoding the message and found a way.

They observed who were the geniuses in the Indian embassy of Moscow who broke the codes. They laid a bait and trapped a person. After that, KGB was able to break all the Indian documents, even those which were not related to the Soviet Union.

During that time, Indian intelligence division, IB was also monitoring KGB's action. Especially, there was a wide spread suspicion that KGB was providing lavish financial support to the Indian Communist Party. But KGB had other tasks in India along with developing communist principles just like in other countries. But IB did not realise it then.

While KGB was strengthening its presence gradually in India, Jawaharlal Nehru who was the prime minister of India died. There was a power war on who would become the next prime minister. In 1964, there were three who were considered as the right fit to become the next prime minister after Nehru— Gulzarilal Nanda, Lal Bahadur Shastri and Morarji Desai.

KGB supported Gulzarilal Nanda among the three. The Soviet Union was ready to support Lal Bahadur Shastri if chances of success for Nanda were less, but they wanted to stop Morarji Desai from becoming the prime minister.

Lal Bahadur Shastri won the contest and became the next prime minister. But his rule did not last for even two years. Following Shastri's sudden death, Nehru's daughter, Indira Gandhi was chosen as the next prime minister.

Similar to Nehru, Indira too believed that the development of Soviet Union was an important event in world history. So, KGB decided that having her as the prime minister would be beneficial to them. So, they provided their complete support and assistance to Indira's government.

Another important point to consider here—just because a few Indian politicians indirectly supported KGB, Gulzarilal Nanda, Lal Bahadur Shastri and Indira Gandhi could not be branded as KGB spies. Mitrokhin mentioned it clearly in his archives.

But, Mitrokhin mentioned that KGB was able to penetrate deep in India only during the rule of Indira Gandhi. When Mitrokhin's archive was released in the format of books, Congress Party was directly affected. Mitrokhin's archive put forth three blames on the Congress rule led by Indira Gandhi:

1. Soviet Union had provided funds for the development of Congress Party. Indira Gandhi had accepted it with or without her knowledge.
2. Similarly, Congress/ Indira Gandhi received funds from American Intelligence agency CIA.
3. A few ministers in Indira's cabinet acted as KGB spies after getting paid by them. They sold government secrets.

Mitrokhin also mentioned that Indira Gandhi might not know about several information like the funds from Russia and the US. The reason was that Lalit Narayan Mishra of her party was the in-charge person for all financial matters. So, Congress Party had received the fund and spent them without knowing the source of the funds, the reason behind or what they expected in return from them. That was also a crime.

In addition to it, Mitrokhin wrote about a few Congress ministers who acted as KGB's secret agents. The numerous information gathered through them was overflowing in KGB's Moscow office.

There is no proof for Mitrokhin's archive apart from the daily notes he had taken. So, this information had to be looked upon as unconfirmed information. Yet, when it was published in the form of a book, several countries including India were shocked.

'Bharatiya Janata Party' requested to launch a detailed investigation about the blame put forth on Indira's rule and Congress. But Congress refused to accept it and ignored it as a fictional book.

Although intense suspense and action are in abundance in the Mitrokhin books, not everything mentioned in it are fictional. At the same time, there is no evidence to prove the events mentioned in it.

So, none of the complaints put forth by Mitrokhin's archive can be proved. Yet, those books are read upon as unconfirmed records of the spy network that KGB had spun throughout the world for more than half a century.

❑

17
Destroyed Dreams

Soviet Union's last president, 'Mikhail Gorbachev' started several reforms which all other presidents either failed to do or hesitated to do.

Mikhail Gorbachev tried to open the gates of the Soviet government which was a closed community since then. He wanted the public to know what happened inside the government. It was people's rule and people had to know what happened inside and there should not be any hidden activities going on.

Although it looks like an interesting effort, the changes Mikhail Gorbachev wanted to bring around in the Soviet Union created shock waves throughout the public. The reason was that since Lenin, all the rulers thrust communism on the people either gently or violently. Although it was described as people's rule, nobody asked what people really wanted or thought.

Mikhail Gorbachev did that. He preferred to analyse the local situation and how to resolve people's problems rather than fighting with the US to prove who has the super power. He invited people to think along with him. That does not mean that Mikhail Gorbachev forgot all his friction with the US and other countries. There were several incidents which prove that he had stood against several countries just to feed his ego.

For example, the British government banished twenty five Soviet citizens from England in 1985 claiming that they were Soviet spies. To retaliate against it, the Gorbachev government chose twenty five British citizens in Russia and banished them. Britain was enraged and sent another five Soviet citizens out of their country. Mikhail Gorbachev did not even flinch and sent five British citizens out of Soviet Union.

Mikhail Gorbachev government's action looked like he was hitting back against other countries whenever Soviet Union citizens were punished on the grounds of espionage. It does not mean that Mikhail Gorbachev supported intelligence activities. He strongly believed that other countries were baiting Soviet Union and its citizens just to spite them. So, he always hit back against such incidents.

The principle followed by Mikhail Gorbachev throughout his rule was simple—Give respect, take respect.

Mikhail Gorbachev was adamant that all the countries including the developed Western countries and third world countries should respect them and to accept them as another superpower. He kept on emphasising that Soviet Union was not lesser than any other superpower country.

In specific, Mikhail Gorbachev requested and received respect that was due to them from the US. During the peace talks between the Soviet Union and US, he efficiently acted without giving up his country's honour and not allowing US to impose their policies and principles upon them.

In August 1986, a person named Gennadi Zakharov was charged as a Soviet spy and was arrested. Several condemnations arose, claiming that the Soviet Union had a dual face with peace talks on one side and intelligence activities on the other side. The Soviet Union government was irritated by it and immediately arrested Nicholas Daniloff, an American journalist who lived in Russia. KGB blamed him of spying on Russia.

Although US and Soviet Union were spiting each other with their childlike behaviour, how did KGB arrest an American reporter all of a sudden as soon as Zakharov was arrested? How did they gather evidence against him so soon?

They did not gather everything instantly. KGB expected such situations to happen and were ready with notes against a few Americans who lived in Russia then. Foreigners living inside the Soviet Union were closely monitored for that. They were researched to find out if they were really spies and even if not, false documents were created against them if needed.

They intentionally sent a local person to become close to them and gave them a few secret documents. Later, they used the same document as evidence and arrested them. Several foreign reporters were caught in that net. It does not mean that all the foreigners who lived in Russia were troubled. But the truth was that if KGB wanted to, anybody could be arrested.

The Mikhail Gorbachev government used KGB for such important tasks during its initial stage. Yet, when his reconstruction plans for Soviet named Perestroika was proposed, he was ready to sacrifice several things which might hinder the plan.

All the reforms which Mikhail Gorbachev wanted to do were new to the people of Soviet Union. But the basic foundation of Perestroika was the principles which were already proposed by Lenin and other communist leaders.

The policies were honourable in real. But Mikhail Gorbachev and his followers believed that they were properly implemented in Soviet Union. There are many who believe that if Lenin did not die so soon and lived longer, he could have made Soviet Union a model country following communist principles.

Mikhail Gorbachev government's Perestroika tried to do the same. Mikhail Gorbachev started to make several reforms including reducing the alcohol usage in Soviet Union, stopping corruption, creating opportunity for everybody to contest in elections, encouraging individual business and several other changes which were never tried by anybody else in the history of the Soviet Union.

Since Mikhail Gorbachev entered into the field without bothering about the effects his reforms might have upon the government agencies, officers and party members, he gained several enemies inside his own country.

Mikhail Gorbachev decided to reduce the powers of KGB as a part of Perestroika. He believed that when a government made by the people and for the people, involves in such severe intelligence activities, people would develop fear and not respect for Soviet Union.

Mikhail Gorbachev's belief was not unlike KGB's then leader, Kryuchkov. But who asked for his opinion?

Several matters which were maintained as a secret by KGB were brought to light under Perestroika. KGB's guardian image started to dim.

Moreover, KGB and Mikhail Gorbachev's reforms did not match in their basic principles. KGB wanted the government to hold the Soviet community within their palms and Gorbachev neglected it as an ancient method.

Kryuchkov was enraged that Mikhail Gorbachev's action had reduced the fear and respect that people had on KGB. He could not reveal his anger directly and hence planned secretly against the government.

There are many who say that Mikhail Gorbachev's 'open' policy to create a huge difference in the lives of everybody from the common man to government officers was the cause of Soviet Union's destruction. So, many were dissatisfied with Mikhail Gorbachev when Perestroika was introduced.

In August 1991, eight important leaders including Kryuchkov joined together and arranged for a protest against Soviet President Mikhail Gorbachev. They planned to force him to retire and take charge of the government. Although Kryuchkov and a few KGB officers directly took part in the protest, it did not yield the result they expected. Their plan against the government failed as a few commanders who were in chief positions stepped back at the last moment.

Many say that the protests against Mikhail Gorbachev faded and disappeared on its own. But, in truth, RSFSR's leader Boris Yeltsin had a great role in breaking the protest. There were problems between Gorbachev and Yeltsin in sharing their authority. But, when he came to know that there was a protest against Gorbachev, he decided to defend Gorbachev and took immediate action to bring the situation under control within a few days.

Although he saved Gorbachev's government, the bad reputation that Soviet Union's own leaders and officers protested against their government became a black mark on the country.

It was the biggest embarrassment in the history of KGB. KGB considered finding and controlling those who acted against the government as its primary mission. But its leader himself had been the chief reason for one such protest.

The next day after the protest, Kryuchkov and others who were involved in the protest were arrested. Vadim Bakatin was chosen as the new leader of KGB to replace Kryuchkov. Other KGB leaders took charge to develop the organisation into a stronger and powerful entity. But Vadim Bakatin became its leader for the sole purpose of closing it.

Bakatin believed in his reforms and decided that an organisation like KGB which held enormous power in its hand was no longer needed for Soviet Union. Kryuchkov's action against the Soviet Union government strengthened his decision further. Once Vadim Bakatin took charge as KGB's leader, its important leaders and members resigned from their post, one by one. By the end of 1991, the entire KGB came under the control of Bakatin.

Following that, buildings and other properties which KGB owned were left to the control of the government based on its location. The Soviet Union security division took charge of all of them.

Not only KGB, but also several Soviet government agencies fell during that period. There were continuous disruptions between the Soviet Union and the Russian government regarding the sharing of power and authority.

When the Soviet Union was formed earlier, it was decided that the countries included in the union can quit from the federation whenever they wanted to. Russia and several other countries wanted to utilise that clause and to move away as a separate country.

Mikhail Gorbachev signed the order to officially dissolve KGB on 24th October 1991. Gorbachev's order came to effect on 6th November . The history of Soviet protection and intelligence organisation started as Cheka just six weeks after Russia's independence came to an end with that order. Within the next few weeks, the Soviet Union was also dissolved on 26th December 1991.

Although the name KGB was not used directly in independent Russia, the responsibilities handled by KGB are being taken care of by a few other organisations.

FSB—Federal Security Service

- This was the organisation which was the direct alternative to KGB, since the fall of Soviet Union in 1991 which was called as Federal Security Service.
- FSK (Federal Counterintelligence Service) was reorganised into FSB in 1995. Mikhail Ivanovich Barsukov was appointed as the head of FSB which was formed as a powerful group with added powers.
- FSB's infrastructure was changed again in 1997. Its size was reduced, power was modified and the importance of other agencies were increased.

SVR—Foreign Intelligence Service

- An individual organisation to handle Russia's foreign intelligence activities, information gathering and research.
- It was the first security division which was equivalent to KGB formed during the fall of the Soviet Union.
- Most of the tasks handled by KGB's 'First Chief Directorate' was handed over to SVR. Yevgeni Primakov was appointed as the head of the organisation.
- After Yevgeni, Vyacheslav Trubnikov served as SVR head from 1996 and Sergei Lebedev from 2000.

FAPSI—Federal Agency of Government Communications and Information

- National security agency which concentrates on communication safety.
- It was formed in 1991 by combining the eighth and sixteenth directorates of KGB.
- Aleksandr Vladimirovich Starovoitov (1991–98), Vladislav Petrovich Sherstyuk (1998–99), Vladimir Georgievich Matykhin (1999–2003) and Yu P Kornev (2003–2010) served as its head.

FSO—Federal Protective service

- Organisation to safeguard Russian national properties and leaders.
- KGB's ninth directorate started to operate as FSO in independent Russia.

KGB, which once operated as a first-class intelligence agency, retired with the same glory. Although its tasks are now broken and shared among several organisations, the memories of the red eagle named KGB left by the 'huge dream', in Soviet Union can never be forgotten.

Appendix 1: KGB – Timeline

- **December 1917–February 1922—Cheka**
  - ★ 20th December 1917—Cheka inauguration, Head—Felix Dzerzhinsky.
  - ★ 1918—Cheka started to operate with Moscow as its headquarters.
  - ★ 19th December 1918—Cheka's special division started for intelligence activities.
  - ★ 1918—Russian Civil War.
  - ★ 20 December 1920— Foreign intelligence agency INO was formed.
  - ★ 1921—Cheka's power was reduced.
  - ★ 6th February 1922—Cheka was dissolved and GPU was formed.

- **February 1922 to July 1923—GPU**
  - ★ 1922—Soviet Union formation.
  - ★ 15th November 1923—GPU was dissolved and OGPU was formed.

- **July 1923 to July 1934—OGPU**
  - ★ 1923—OGPU was recognised as an individual commission.
  - ★ 1926—Felix died and Vyacheslav Rudolfovich Menzhinsky became the new leader.
  - ★ 1930—Organisation to manage Gulag (concentration camps) was formed.
  - ★ 1930—Soviet Politburo decided to intensify intelligence in Britain, France and Germany.
  - ★ 1934—Menzhinsky died and Genrikh Grigoryevich Yagoda became the leader.

- ★ 1934—OGPU was dissolved and its responsibilities were handed over to GUGB.

- **July 1934 to February 1946—NKVD**
  - ★ 1937—Yagoda's arrest, Nikolai Ivanovich Yezhov became the new leader.
  - ★ 1938—New leader Lavrenty Pavlovich Beria.

- **1934 to 1941—GUGB of the NKVD**

- **April 1943 to March 1946—NKGB**
  - ★ 1943—SMERSH intelligence agency was formed.

- **March 1946 to October 1953—MGB**

- **October 1947 to November 1951—KI (foreign intelligence division)**
  - ★ 1947—MGB and GRU were merged.
  - ★ 1948—GRU went back under the control of defence ministry.

- **1946 to 1954—MVD**
  - ★ 1953—MGB and MVD collaborated.
  - ★ 1953—Beria was arrested Sergei Nikiforovich Kruglov was the new leader.
  - ★ 1954—MVD's powers were reduced. Lost the ministry.

- **March 1954 to October 1991—KGB**
  - ★ 13 March 1954—KGB formation, new leader was Ivan Alexandrovich Serov.
  - ★ 1958—KGB's new leader was Alexander Nikolayevich Shelepin.

★ 1961—KGB's new leader was Vladimir Yefimovich Semichastny.

★ 1967—KGB's new leader was Yuri Vladimirovich Andropov. KGB strengthened both politically and systemically.

★ 1978—Name changed to Soviet Union KGB.

★ 1982—Yuri Vladimirovich Andropov became the president of Soviet Union. KGB's new leader was Viktor Chebrikov.

★ 1984—Cheka/KGB museum was formed.

★ 1991—KGB leader's protest against Mikhail Gorbachev's government failed.

★ 1991—Kryuchkov's arrest. KGB's new leader Vadim Bakatin.

★ 6thNovember 1991—KGB was dissolved.

★ 26th December 1991—Soviet Union was dissolved.

- **Backstory**

  ★ 1992—Former KGB document keeper Mitrokhin moved to Britain. The documents collected by him are smuggled into Britain.

  ★ 1999—Mitrokhin archive's first part got released and raised uproar.

  ★ Important organisations which perform tasks equivalent to KGB in independent KGB: FSB & SVR.

Appendix 2: KGB – Structure

- **KGB's important directorates:**

  ★ First Primary directorate—directorate responsible for foreign action and intelligence tasks.

- ★ Second directorate —internal affairs including internal politics, Soviet people and foreigners inside Soviet.
- ★ Third directorate—armed forces surveillance and military counter-intelligence.
- ★ Fourth directorate—transportation security.
- ★ Fifth directorate—internal safety, monitoring and audit.
- ★ Sixth directorate—economic counter-intelligence, industrial security.
- ★ Seventh directorate—monitoring local/foreign citizens, supervision.
- ★ Eighth directorate—communication (local/foreign), improving related technologies).
- ★ Ninth directorate—uniformed bodyguards protecting leaders, their families and national properties.
- ★ Fifteenth directorate—safeguarding government agencies.
- ★ Sixteenth directorate—Telephone and telegram services.

- **Other important divisions:**
  - ★ Personnel department
  - ★ Administration
  - ★ Finance department
  - ★ Archives
  - ★ Border Guards

Appendix 3: Books/Articles/Magazines

- **Books:**

  - ★ Robert M Slusser, Simon Wolin & Frederick A Praeger—*The Soviet Secret Police*. Research Program on the USSR, 1957

- Christopher Andrew, Vasili Mitrokhin—*The Sword and the Shield: The Mitrokhin Archive and the Secret History of the KGB.* Basic Books, 2001
- Christopher Andrew, Vasili Mitrokhin—*The Mitrokhin Archives II: The KGB and the World.* , 1984
- Martin Ebon—*KGB: Death and Rebirth.* Praeger Publishers, 1994
- Peter Kenez—A History of the Soviet Union from the Beginning to the End. Cambridge University Press, 1999
- Nicholas Daniloff—*Two Lives, One Russia*. Avon Books, 1990
- ரஷ்யப்புரட்சி: ஒருபுதியதரிசனம் - என். ராமகிருஷ்ணன் - கிழக்குபதிப்பகம், 2006
- 8. மதேினம் - கே. சலெ்வப்பரெுமாள் - பாரதிபுத்தகாலயம, 2005

- **Articles:**
  - Gareth Jones— 'OGPU'S Reign of Terror in Russia'. *The Western Mail*, 1933
  - Oliver Henry Radkey—'The Election to the Russian Constituent Assembly of 1917'. Harvard University Press, 1950
  - E H Curr—'The Origin and Status of the Cheka'. Soviet Studies, 1958
  - David Wallechinsky, Irving Wallace— 'The KGB'. Trivia Library, 1981
  - Patricia Blake— 'A Top Cop Takes the Helm'. Time, 1982
  - Patricia Blake—'Changing the Guard'. Time, 1982
  - Victor Herman, Fred E Dohrs— 'In Stalin's Footsteps: Yuri Andropov: Rise of a Dictator'. Library Haven, Journal of Hillsdale College, 1983

- George J Church—'Men of the Year: Ronald Reagan & Yuri Andropov'. Time, 1984
- Aileen O'Carroll—'The Cheka during the Russian revolution'. Workers Solidarity Movement, 1992
- Natalia Gevorkian—'The KGB: They still need us'. Bulletin of the Atomic Scientists, 1993
- Eric Lee—'The Eremin Letter'. Revolutionary Russia,1993
- Michael I Schwartz— 'The Russian-American Bomb: The Role of Espionage in the Soviet Atomic Bomb Project'. History of Science, 1996
- John Pike—'Committee for State Security'. FAS Intelligence Resource Program, 1997
- Stephen Dalziel—'Russia: 80 Murky Years of the KGB'. BBC, 1997
- History of the ChK OGPU NKVD KGB, T, CyberUSSR, 1998
- J Michael Waller—'The Secret History of the KGB'. Insight on the News, 1999
- Vasiliy Mitrokhin—'How to be a KGB spy'. *The Guardian,* 2002
- Dr Dennis F Casey—'Lawful terror: The Cheka'. *Spokesman*, 2002
- Kuldip Nayar—'All are naked in the bath'. *Deccan Herald*, 2005
- மீத்ரோகின்ஆவணங்கள் - பத்ரிசேஷாத்ரி - http://thoughtsintamil.blogspot.com/ - 2005
- மாயவலை - பா. ராகவன்குமுதம்ரிப்போர்ட்டர் - 2006
- உஷார்உளவாளி - சுதாங்கன்ஜூனியர்விகடன் - 2006
- Mesrob Vartavarian—'The NKVD'. NKVD.org

★ Oleg Khlevnyuk—'The Economy of the OGPU, NKVD and MVD of the USSR'

- **Websites:**
  - ★ http://cr.middlebury.edu/public/russian/Bulgakov/public_html//NKVD.html
  - ★ http://en.wikipedia.org/
  - ★ http://english.pravda.ru/
  - ★ http://experts.about.com/
  - ★ http://flag.blackened.net/revolt/talks/cheka.html
  - ★ http://home.sandiego.edu/~landeros/KGBCIA/KGB.htm
  - ★ http://iaia.essortment.com/cheka_rvph.htm
  - ★ http://library.thinkquest.org/10826/kgb.htm
  - ★ http://news.bbc.co.uk/2/hi/world/analysis/41319.stm
  - ★ http://thoughtsintamil.blogspot.com/
  - ★ http://users.skynet.be/terrorism/
  - ★ http://www.answers.com/
  - ★ http://www.cnn.com/
  - ★ http://www.country-data.com/
  - ★ http://www.cyberussr.com/
  - ★ http://www.everything2.com/
  - ★ http://www.fas.org/irp/world/russia/kgb/index.html
  - ★ http://www.findarticles.com/p/articles/mi_m1571/is_37_15/ai_56184189
  - ★ http://www.geocities.com/CapitolHill/2808/chap3.html
  - ★ http://www.google.com/
  - ★ http://www.guardian.co.uk/saturday_review/story/0,3605,643341,00.html
  - ★ http://www.historyguide.org/europe/cheka.html
  - ★ http://www.ibiblio.org/expo/soviet.exhibit/secret.html

- ★ http://www.libertyhaven.com/
- ★ http://www.mosnews.com/
- ★ http://www.nkvd.org/
- ★ http://www.npr.org/templates/story/story.php?storyId=4948068
- ★ http://www.pbs.org/redfiles/kgb/deep/kgb_deep_ref_detail.htm
- ★ http://www.periclespress.com/Russia_KGB.html
- ★ http://www.questia.com/library/kgb.jsp
- ★ http://www.reference.com/
- ★ http://www.rusnet.nl/encyclo/k/kgb.shtml
- ★ http://www.spartacus.schoolnet.co.uk/
- ★ http://www.st-andrews.ac.uk/
- ★ http://www.thebulletin.org/article.php?art_ofn=jf93gevorkian
- ★ http://www.timesonline.co.uk/
- ★ http://www.tiscali.co.uk/reference/encyclopaedia/hutchinson/m0014072.html
- ★ http://www.trivia-library.com/b/history-of-russian-government-agency-the-kgb-part-1.htm
- ★ http://www.uh.edu/~vlazarev/4389/Gulag-khlev.htm
- ★ http://www.xs4all.nl/~kvenjb/madmonarchs/ivan4/ivan4_bio.htm
- ★ https://www.cia.gov/csi/books/17240/art-3.html

- **Magazines/Newspapers**
  - ★ *The Guardian*
  - ★ *Pravda*

❑❑❑